UNDERNOSE
FARM
REVISITED

HARRY CROSBIE OBE is best known
as the developer who transformed
Dublin and its music scene during the
late 1980s and 1990s with the Point
and Bord Gáis theatres, Vicar Street
and the docklands. His voice will leave
an equal mark on cultural memory.

FOR RITA, CLAIRE,
ALISON, SIMON

UNDERNOSE FARM REVISITED

Harry Crosbie

THE LILLIPUT PRESS
DUBLIN

First published 2021 by

THE LILLIPUT PRESS LTD
62–63 Sitric Road, Arbour Hill, Dublin 7, Ireland
www.lilliputpress.ie

ISBN 978 1 84351 815 0

A CIP record is available from the British Library.

1 3 5 7 9 10 8 6 4 2

Set in 12pt on 17pt Scala by Niall McCormack
Printed in County Kerry

CONTENTS

I

I I

UNDERNOSE
FARM
REVISITED

I

1

EIGHTEEN AND A HALF

Adventure. You want adventure? I'll give you adventure.

I was eighteen and a half, my mother told me I was gorgeous. Long black hair down my back, stiff-legged walk like Gene Pitney on the telly. Could not care less: cool – no, I mean *totally* cool; cool as the Lone Ranger.

It was 1965, I had left school, burnt the books, it was a long summer. I was ready, man!

I had been in a skiffle group with Fran O'Toole from Bray. I was a Bengal – chancer to you – but he was a naturally gifted musician, bastard. I went to see him in my uncle's Morris Minor van. His father owned a bingo hall. At that time, English mill workers still came to Bray for their holidays. Mad or what?

Girls, girls, girls everywhere. One quiet afternoon the manager was sick (i.e. drunk) and I got to call out the bingo. Totally cool.

I did it real slow. Smouldering. My bird was up the front: cheeky, cowboy hat, fringes, factory girl – classy. Boy heaven. See you later, alligator, I said with my eyes.

There was a phone outside Fran's house. Press Button B, sickly green. I had promised to call a new friend, a hippy head from Bray, otherwise known as The Bray Head. Fur coat, beads, no socks: cool.

'Hey, man,' he said.

'Hey, man,' I said.

'Have you got £65?' he asked.

'No bother,' I said.

I had £12, my communion money. My granny was minding it, but my sisters were loaded and an easy touch.

'I'm gonna hitch to the Middle East,' he said.

'Cool,' I said, 'Good weed there, man.'

'Wanna come?' he asked.

'Does Dolly Parton sleep on her back?' Boys of eighteen should be chained to a radiator until their brains switch on.

'The mail boat is Friday, 7 pm,' The Head said.

'Bring it on.'

'We travel light,' he said. 'One rucksack only.'

'I don't have a rucksack.'

'Capel Street, Cheeky Charlie's,' he said.

I told my mother I was going to see a friend for a few days. She packed a little case for me with beautifully ironed pyjamas, hankies, socks, all tied in bows with green silk ribbons. She gave me a box of chocs for my friend's mother. Silk bows – what's that about?

It was a rough crossing. We drank eight pints with a crowd of Irish tinkers/horse dealers ... don't ask.

I threw the little case with its bows into an angry sea and gave the chocs to a couple of drunken girls. Cruel, cruel youth.

After a rain-sodden week of misery we got to a small German town. We stayed in the local dosshouse. 'Keep your hand on your halfpenny,' my granny told me.

We put the two end-legs of the bed into our boots and our money under the legs nearest the wall. There was a long row of beds, all with boots on. It was a funny, sad sight.

In the Munich beer halls we heard that Dachau was just outside the city. A group of us went next day. It really does say *'Arbeit Macht Frei'* on the gate. Then a strange and frightening thing happened. I could not go through the gate and into the camp – some sense of evil or force of remembered suffering stopped me like a blow in the chest. I waited outside for two hours. They laughed at me as they went in. There was no laughing coming out.

We were on the road to Istanbul, hippie head office for we alternative folk – property is theft. We hitched a big trailer truck heading for Syria. My war-comic German stood me in good stead. *'Wann ist der nächte Lastwagen, bitte?'* I asked. I told the Arab driver, my new friend, that my father was a capitalist and had trucks, and that I could drive heavy machinery.

Night fell, an empty moon hung over an empty desert road. He asked me to drive. The Bray Head was asleep in the bunk. The driver was impressed, up and down the gearbox, no bother. Dancing!

He rolled a spliff and then it happened: talking sweet and low, he put his hand on my leg (upper). I pushed it away and told him to stop. Nothing more for an hour. He was drinking whiskey, didn't offer me any. The mood darkened. Driving a big truck with blazing headlights on a moonlit desert road is a calm and beautiful thing. Eating up the miles, Arab music softly on the radio. Quiet. Then the hand again, upper upper, this time no sweet talk. I braked hard and pulled in with squealing tyres and a dust cloud. I cut the big diesel, sudden silence except the ticking of a cooling engine in the cold desert night air. I turned towards the bunk and shouted at The Bray Head to scarper.

We jumped down from the cab and rolled in between the trailer axles: I told you I was good with trucks. The driver stood out in the headlamp beams casting a long shadow into the desert. He had a heavy wrench in his hand and was looking for us. Not a happy camper. I put a finger to my lips to tell The Bray Head to keep shtumm. It turned out he did not believe in fighting or war. Spare me – pacifism has its time and place. More likely he was a cowardy, cowardy custard.

I crawled along the chassis to the sow-belly box – again, don't ask – and got a steel pin. The driver had no night vision due to the blazing lamps. I ran out of the darkness and hit him hard. He went down like the proverbial. Lights out. 'Not tonight, Josephine,' I said. Good line under the circs, I thought.

I switched off the truck's lights and we walked all night, hiding from any traffic. We stayed for a week to 'rest up', as the cowboys say. Thessaloniki. Nice town, you should try it.

We stayed in the youth hostel. I met a beautiful blonde English girl. I know she fancied me as she completely ignored me and never looked at me. Girls and their little tricks, eh? One night we were all sitting out in the yard rolling our 'Soviet' spliff. Everyone puts in their gear, a forty-Rizla paper job, eighteen inches long. My new bird was kissing another bloke in front of me so I knew I was in. Oh, the games we play.

People don't give blood in Thessaloniki, they sell it. We sold our blood every day for five local dollars a litre. More money than God. I sent flip-flops to my mother. They would be handy for her around the house, I thought.

Then we heard there was a big dope dealer paying twenty dollars for European blood. Four Germans from our hostel said they would go and check it out. They did not turn up for our 'Soviet' that evening.

Early next morning I was in my *Schlafsack* (German again) up on the roof of the hostel. I woke to a heavy kick of a boot. Four policemen stood around me. Not a good start to one's day.

'Do you smoke dope?' one asked.

'Never,' I said.

'Have you got any dope now?' another asked.

'Definitely not,' I said. I gently moved my stash to the end of my *Schlafsack* with my foot.

'Do you know the four persons who left here last night?'

'Yes,' I said, 'they were Herman the German and his gang ... I mean group. We were expecting them home for our evening sing-song.'

'They are not coming back,' one said.

'Oh?' I said.

'Yes,' said another, 'they went to an illegal blood dealer. We found them lying on the beds still hooked up to the tubes. They had all the blood in their bodies drained completely.'

'Drained?' I said.

'Yes,' they said. 'Completely.'

'Are they all right?' I said.

'No, they are not all right, they are all dead. All four. Dead.'

My brain froze. I saw only my mother's beautifully ironed pyjamas with the little green bows.

I began to cry. I wanted to go home to her right then and beg her forgiveness. I wanted to fold her in my arms and touch her hair and tell her I had left as a stupid, stupid boy but now I was a man. I wanted to tell her I would do something every day of my life from now on to make her happy. I wanted to sit and eat buttery toast with her in the mornings. I wanted to tell her that now I understood her love and cherished it. I wanted to tell her I would bring her in our Morris Minor van to her favourite place in the world, a little seaside hotel in Wexford where she and my father got married. We would go for a paddle in the patient, gentle sea as we had always done on our summer holidays, before I grew up and became a man.

2
WALKING ON WATER

Mattie was a small man, a really small man, less than five feet tall. He had a big flat head and the local joke was that it would be a handy place to set down your pint when the pub was busy. Mattie was an inventor, artist, mechanic, designer, welder, carpenter, fitter, and he played the fiddle.

He walked on water: repeat, walked on water.

He was from a small village on the Shannon. He craved adventure as a young man and declared to the village that he would walk across the Shannon. He invented a pair of floating boots. These were five feet long, the same as himself. They were bright red with laces neatly tied and bowed. Long laces. Mattie explained that red was a navigational aid to ensure safety to other river traffic. Each boot had a rod standing up roughly where the big toe was located. This was connected to a flat board below, which led across the sole of the boot. When a step forward was taken the rod was pushed down so that the board dropped and bit into the water.

Traction, you see. In this fashion, he stood as if he had two walking sticks as well as being slightly drunk and/or crippled. He moved forward with slow, giant moonwalker steps.

The first three attempts failed. The starboard boot filled with water and Mattie developed a list. The support vessel, his cousin in a rowing boat, took the boot on board and towed Mattie ashore. Running repairs. Push on, his mantra; push on.

By this time word had spread far and wide. The next Sunday there was another attempt – think the conquest of Everest. Clear weather, no wind. Perfect conditions. A small crowd gathered. The local paper took Mattie's picture. The priest blessed the boots. Prayers.

This time the boots did him proud. He set off to a ragged cheer. Giant step forward, push rod down. Repeat. He worked up a rhythm. Step, push down. Step, push down. Step, push down. Repeat. Repeat. Repeat. The crowd sensed he was going to make it, or die trying. They surged across the bridge to form a welcoming committee on the other bank.

A few tense moments mid-stream on the mighty river. The crowd held its breath. Our hero struggled. Drown or win. Do or die. What drama, what a day out for a little village. Women remembered what they wore on that outing.

He stepped on to dry land and into history. His own small girlfriend rushed forward, the soldier she'd left him for forgotten – but that ship had sailed. Women.

What is it with women and heroes? The world was now his lobster. Form an orderly queue.

Mattie drove a Morris Minor van with a large roof rack and many toolboxes. He always carried a collapsible canvas canoe, securely lashed down. He canoed during his lunch hour, winter and summer, no matter where he was. He was a flask-and-sandwiches man. His canoe design was an advance on the wartime Cockleshell Heroes special commando force, his heroes. He constantly refined his design for a four-bladed paddle to improve efficiency. He also rode a 500cc Triumph motorbike at full speed. His joke was that his bike was mentioned in the Bible: 'Jesus rode in his Triumph across the desert.'

His business was the operation of a low-loader. He took on only difficult and wide loads. This involved much measuring and rough sketching. He liked things that were complicated and difficult. HEAVY HAULAGE, it said on his gate. He carried a tape at all times and measured the things around him constantly.

My father used to go for a quiet pint with him. They were pals. My father knew how wise he was. They were banished to the yard of the pub as he smoked a huge, curved pipe. This required an array of small knives and tools to keep it lit, sometimes even pliers. Clouds of smoke signalled success like the announcement of the election of a new pope in the Vatican. He drank only sherry. No one knew why. He swore by it. 'Mother's milk,' he called it.

He told my father he was unlucky in love and spoke of his lady friend, one of the few women west of the Shannon smaller than himself. His broken heart told him it was the soldier's uniform she'd left him for. Because he could love no other, he gave his life to inventing.

One day my father came home full of news. Mattie was working on a new challenge, navigating the Royal Canal from the Liffey west to the Shannon. This was long before pleasure boating had begun. The canals were decayed and derelict. The basin at Grand Canal quay was known locally as the Forgotten Pond.

I was offered a position as a 'nipper' on what was to be an 'epic attempt'. History called. Think Sherpa Tenzing. My mother said, 'No son of mine is going to sea with that half-mad midget,' and downed tools.

The plan was to buy a lifeboat from a dredger that was being scrapped in the Liffey dockyards. My father knew the man. It was the Dublin way. We'd take it to Mattie's yard and build *accommodation* and a *wheelhouse*. The work was to take one month. I would be paid £1 per week as a *junior rating*. Royal Navy terms were now standard.

The voyage was to take two weeks. On Mattie's arrival at the Shannon, ladies would be invited for pleasure-cruising on the lakes for a short time. Then the vessel was to be burnt, Viking-style, in the middle of the river, as an offering to the gods.

Words turned into action. An ancient lifeboat, 26ft long, clinker-built, timber, was bought for £50 with a

£10 bung for the lads. It was transported on Mattie's low-loader to the yard. We fell to work. I found salt tablets and hard biscuits from the war under the seat. Exciting. The biscuits were tough as rocks but lovely dunked into a nice cup of tea. We were eating history. The vessel was named *Loretta*, after a lady friend.

During the day, when Mattie was out working, I scraped down the hull. The party wall with the old cinema next door allowed me to share intimate moments of ecstasy with a woman loudly confirming approval of her lover's efforts following a shoot-out in which he had saved her from certain death. By the time the boat – sorry – *vessel* was ready I knew every line and every moan of pleasure in the picture. The old yard man thought she was faking it. It sounded good to me.

By the time I was putting the kettle on for our afternoon tea and cake the soundtrack through the wall had turned into flying crockery and screams of 'The bitch, I'll scratch her eyes out!' My mother said, when I was quizzed, 'So unlike the home life of our own dear Queen.' She and her sister went to see the film, to confirm it was filth and the woman was a hussy.

The little engine was stripped down and lovingly rebuilt. It was started to test on the bench, and all agreed it was as sweet as a nut and ran like a sewing machine. No higher praise. Mattie worked on the *superstructure* (plywood cabin) far into the night, listening to the romance and strife next door during the evening show. We never asked him if he felt she was faking it.

Because of the gossip, the yard attracted attention. We had a break-in. Heavies. The usual: tyres, copper, brass, next week's wages. I discovered this when I opened the warehouse and found the two yard Alsatians, Winston and Margaret, hanging dead from ropes twenty-five feet up in the air under broken skylights. The heavies had dropped rope lassoes onto the ground and put meat in the centre. As the dogs ate, they pulled the noose tight and hanged them high. We buried them under a bed of nettles. Mattie, me and the yardman cried.

To get to the yard I had to pass a gang of Teddy boys standing outside the cinema. By this time word had leaked of the attempt and my role in it.

'Is Mattie bringing the other six?' I was asked.

'Will you have women in every town?'

'Are you out or on a message?'

I walked past with my Marmite sandwiches and shouted back, 'I have two big brothers!' It was my mother they should be afraid of. But real Teddy boys at that time were hard men, with razorblades in their lapels.

The big day dawned. Sunday morning. Empty streets. A small convoy set out from the yard to the canal lock for the launch. Mattie, of course, had his own crane. The truck was marked DANGEROUS LOAD.

We arrived at the launch site. The crane and slings were set up. The low-loader was backed into position. The lift began. My job was to remain on board to catch a rope *mid-steam* to secure the *vessel*. Our *provisions* (sandwiches) had been laid out: biscuit tins lined up, rubber bands holding the lids shut. Each was marked Lock 1, Lock 2, Lock 3 etc. I realized I was eating the Mullingar sandwiches. Should I tell Mattie? Would we be able to get food down the country?

When I looked out, we were above the trailer and swinging out over the lock. Much shouting and pointing. The *vessel* slowly, slowly sank below the wall and gently settled on the water. We were afloat. The slings went slack. A wonderful, light-as-air sensation. Mattie beamed with excitement. I was rearranging the Mullingar sandwiches with the Ashtown sandwiches when I felt water lapping at my ankles. I was wondering what this meant when I heard shouts from the quayside.

'You're sinking, you're sinking! Jump for your life!'

I froze. The Ashtown sandwiches fell into the water. The *vessel* was going down fast. I climbed out onto the roof of the *superstructure*. The boat settled on the bottom of the canal at an angle. I was left in the middle of the canal on one square foot of plywood, surrounded by water. I could feel the boat still moving. Tricky. Time for a cool head.

Mattie, ashen-faced, shouted: 'Keep calm, do not move a muscle! I have a plan.'

He jumped into the crane and swung the hook out over me. I grabbed a hold and was hoisted through the air and landed ashore. It was like something in a war movie. My finest hour. If only my pals could see me. Bravest of the brave.

We regrouped.

My mother had heard what was going on and there she was. I tried to explain to her that this was no place or time for a woman and got a clip round the ear in front of my fellow crew members. The shame, the shame.

She pulled Mattie's cap off and threw it into the canal. 'Mad old bastard!' she shouted.

She caught me by the ear, like in the *Beano*, and dragged me home.

'I'm a man,' I said.

'You're a brat,' she said.

Back at home I was put to bed. The doctor was called. 'There's nothing wrong with me!' I shouted down the stairs.

'You're in shock,' she shouted back. 'You may have fleas.'

'My crew need me, I want to stay with my men!' I shouted again.

My father had gone into hiding. This meant he was drinking in a strange pub and might as well be on the moon.

The rest of my story can only be told second-hand. Me and my father were barred from Mattie's yard. For ever.

'Mad dwarf bastard!' she said over and over. 'My beautiful son, left stranded on the sea.'

I tried to explain that the canal was not the sea, and got another clip on the ear.

Poor Mattie salvaged his failed boat alone. He could explain: it was a rotten plank, squeezed by the hoist.

Push on. Fail again, fail better. But there was no push on. No girls in every town.

'Remember the *Titanic!*' the Teddy boys shouted. 'Can Grumpy swim?'

He retired to his yard a broken man. He went back to inventing. He built a huge radio mast and learnt Morse code. He made many new friends around the world. His call sign, or handle, was 'Walk on water'. His new friends would never know from the *dot-dash-dot* streaming across the night skies of the world's oceans that they were dealing with a hero. But I knew, and Mattie knew I knew.

3

WHY DO BEES DANCE?

Hibo was a casual day-labourer who stood waiting for work every morning at the dock gates. If there was no work, a large crowd of men went home with nothing, or went to the dockside pub to drink on the slate. Truckers picked up men to land cargo 'under the hook' from working ships.

I was a boy on school holidays: my job was to drive a pick-up and hire men for our loading. Hibo was a regular and we became unlikely friends. He had a strangeness and sadness in him. He stood apart from the group. He was born into the savage poverty of a 1930s Dublin tenement. He lived on the street, tough and hard as nails. He sang softly or whistled. He rarely spoke.

At sixteen he joined the British army to get away from a violent, murderous father. He went to war and was captured by the Japanese at the fall of Singapore. He spent the war working on the Burma death railway. His job was to bury the dead. If the track was building over stony ground and it was too hard to dig, they burnt a pile of corpses each morning with petrol.

He received many brutal beatings, which happened when a prisoner caught the eye of a guard. All prisoners had to look down when a guard was present. He survived the war, but was damaged physically and hurt spiritually.

When he came home, he lived in the Iveagh lodgings if he had work and the price of a bed. If not, he slept rough winter and summer.

Before the coming of containers, dockside work was hard labour. Cranes landed heavy hoists of sacks and cargo onto trailer beds, to be laid out as a safe load. 'Let the weight do the work,' was the advice. Swing the sack loosely. Lift gently, move slowly, keep a rhythm, keep legs soft and bend. Steady. Never stand under a swinging hoist. Work, watch, wait.

Some Saturday mornings after pay-out I went for a walk with Hibo and his friend John; a ramble, they called it. It was always the same. First port of call – the stones market in Cumberland Street. Second-hand coats and boots sold off the cobblestones. Women fitted and fussed over the men like mothers with small boys. Much coarse laughing. You would not want to be shy or easily shocked. I was asked, was I a virgin? Mary could soften my cough. Have you dropped yet, son. Scarlet.

Next up – the Flying Angel sailors' rest. White-pudding sandwiches and a big mug of hot, sweet tea. Crews from every nation, every colour, every creed. Broken English, sometimes singing, even in the morning. Photos passed around of much-missed families; crowds of children and small, unsmiling women. The odd tear, brown faces twisted in loneliness. Years away at sea, wages sent home to distant villages.

Always, the Liffey ferry across the river to Sir John Rogerson's Quay. The ferryman was a local hero. 'Good-looking women free,' he shouted up, 'pregnant woman down the back.' A good sob story always worked. 'I'll pay you next week.'

'No bother. We know where you live.'

As the ferry set out: 'Bring us back a parrot.'

The steel hull banged hard against the towering granite blocks. Greasy, dangerous, steep steps. It was good to get up to dry land and the warm sun. The river was not to be trusted.

Then a walk to the Iveagh Baths in Tara Street where the *Irish Times* building is now. My friends showed me one of Dublin's secret places. Up and over the pool and its squealing kids, a quiet corridor was lined on each side with doors of dimpled, frosted glass. Each opened into a clean, bare room with a large, deep white bath with heavy brass taps. The man handed out a rough towel and a bar of carbolic soap. He filled the bath to the top with scalding water. There was no chat here. Men sat on wooden benches in the hall, reading in silence. It was a peaceful and private place, the noise of the main pool muffled and far away.

I was too young to be let in so I waited across the street in a café. My friends came out transformed. They were relaxed and happy. It was the high point of their week. I learned many years later that not only poor people used the baths – many professional men went to that calm and secret place.

In the café, before we parted, Hibo and John would tell stories of the war. A British officer, much liked, gave English lessons to Indian troops based on the story of 'Why Bees Dance'. It is because they have done their work well, collected their pollen, and dance and wiggle with happiness and delight. 'A lesson for us all,' the officer would say, 'a lesson for us all.' The whole class did the wiggle dance and never forgot.

Another secret, which shames me to this day. Hibo and John had nowhere to go as the hostel did not open until six o'clock. They would walk to Dalkey or Howth to stay out of the pub and keep their money for the hostel. Meanwhile I went home to my mother for my tea and a warm fire.

School started up again and I did not see Hibo for nearly a year. At Christmas he had failed in health and looked thin and worn.

At home one day my father was upset and agitated. He told us that men would call to the door and we were to stay away. It was Hibo and John who came. They carried a small white box with a dead infant in it. My father drove them to Glasnevin, where they buried the little white box in the angel plot. My father had arranged it with a gravedigger he knew from the pub. All day my mother cried her heart out and clung to me fiercely. She did not let me out of her sight.

A bitter cold winter morning with roads heavily frosted and dangerous. I was opening up the yard for an early start. Along the wall of a warehouse stood a row of heavy timber hogsheads to catch the rainwater from the vast slate warehouse roof. Around one of the hogsheads lay chunks of ice and in it, Hibo, sitting in the water, only his head showing with his cap on, just above the icy water. He had been there most of the night. He stopped his soft singing to wish me good morning. He said it was too hot in the jungle and he was cooling down.

Two older drivers lifted him out of the freezing water. He was naked except for his cap, painfully thin and white as a boy. The men wrapped their coats around him and carried him into the office. He was sat in front of a big electric fire. The medical chest was broken open for the brandy. I made him hot, sweet tea. He told me I was the only person who had ever been kind to him. He told me it was one of the best times of his life when I got him to tell me the dancing bees story over and over because I loved it so much. We did the wiggle dance. My father and a driver put him into warm, dry clothes and brought him in a small van to Grangegorman mental asylum. He was put to bed where he slept for three days and nights.

Some weeks later Hibo started work as a cleaner in the asylum bakery. The old pals act from the pub had got him this plum job. My father called to see him. He said he loved the routine and security, tending the big ovens, happy as a baby. The whole bakery shone with his work.

The following Christmas a package arrived, beautifully wrapped in pristine, heavy brown paper and tied with twine. Government issue. In it were a loaf of bread and a small, plain cake. The note was from Hibo. I knew it was written by another hand, as he could not write.

I am happy for the first time in my life, he said. *I am content and love my work. I have been promoted to trainee baker and this is my first loaf. I will bless each loaf I make for your good fortune. I put my war medal into the little cake. I hope you will remember me when you see it. I hope you will visit me when you are old enough to get in. Bring a white pudding and I will bake bread for a sandwich for you. I hope you will remain my friend.*

He died in the winter of that year. He was buried in an unmarked grave with not one living soul present. He had no family and as we had no official connection to him we were not informed of his death.

Hibo had a hard, cruel life, marked only by a cheap, mass-produced medal he won fighting in a war he did not understand and which had nothing to do with him. But his life touched the hearts of one family. His medal is minded, and the one small photo of him that we have is carefully kept in our biscuit tin. This must make him part of the family, and maybe that's enough.

4

DIPSTICK DAY

Saturday morning, payday. Men looked forward to it. It was not work. It was a gathering of men for men.

An old yard by the river: trucks, cranes, trailers, cargo, workshops. A place of work. An oil drum punched with the square holes of a pickaxe. Timber burning inside. Three more oil drums lashed together in a shamrock shape surrounded by pallet seating for thirty men. Friends and comrades. Each man knew the other. Good and bad, fights forgotten. Friends.

Boiling, blackened kettles, teapots, ancient cracked mugs. Tea leaves in twists of paper, milk in old Baby Power bottles.

Each man shyly put in little packets of sweet cake, a slice or two of apple tart, some biscuits. All to share. Jokes about the wife's cooking. Cigarettes stabbed out, stabbers behind ear. No smoking during eating. Some men took their caps off and put them on their knee, a strange gesture, no longer seen.

Older men wore the jacket of their good suit. They were treated with deference. This was a time to be marked. There was an air of gentleness. Men behaved kindly one to another. Kindly is a strange word to use for men gathered, but kindly it was.

A man took off his boots and pulled out the laces to show a yard boy how to lace his work boots properly and safely. I watched. I repeat it to this day. Knowledge handed down. Those iron-muscled hands could lash down a cargo with secret knots that would endure the storms of seven seas and not stir. Yet they were gentle this day.

Most work was piece-rate and led by the daily port 'read'. No work, no pay. No books. No cheque. No guff. Cash. Nelson Eddies, readies. Saturday morning. Every week.

Each name called out from the office. Each man strode up importantly for his wages. Pride was there. Quick tot agreed. Money slapped down. Silver lined up in little green, red, brown bank bags with little punch holes in the sides. Quick look at the pretty girl in the office. She had more power than she would ever know.

Walk back to fire, money comfortable in pocket. Smiles, I remember, big smiles.

One or two of the men had ramshackle old cars. These were much admired. A star turn in the centre of the yard, always with the bonnet up. It is a truth universally acknowledged that men love looking into an engine. After a wash by many willing hands, it was time for the magic ritual of the oil check. When the oil settled (much discussion of this point) the owner – and only the owner – slowly, dramatically took out the dipstick and displayed it on a clean rag for all to see, its mystery open to the light. The little ogham lines told their secret story. All was well. The matador slid back his sword to fight again another day. A sigh of satisfaction in the group. Job well done. Talk of oil pressure, mileage, icy roads. All conquered. Someday soon they would buy a car, a Ford. Your only man. No nonsense. Would run on the smell of an oily rag.

Fire put out. Sweep yard. Ready to go to pub. Will there be work next week? God is good.

Black, foaming pints bought in rounds, hidden friendships laid down from long before time remembering. The good manners of a new large Player's offered with the clean snap of cellophane and one cigarette eased forward for your friend to take. A small, quick cave of light in cupped hands. Blue words. Fathers nodded to sons, all good, all good.

After the pub, the toss school. A local green space. A hundred men tightly packed. The tosser, Willyboy, with two halfpennies on a small flat stick. Throw into the air, higher than a house. Tumbling, splitting the light. Heads or tails, odds or evens. Win or lose, winner take all. A shouting circle of men formed by outstretched arms, each man holding back the other. Heads back, faces to the sky. Shouting as they fell back to earth. Then, the appalling truth of life laid bare for all to see. It's all random chance. Pure luck or lack of it. Winners shouting, losers silent. Bets paid out. Told you I felt lucky today. It was ever thus. We are all spinning halfpennies in the air, to fall face up or face down. Life.

Then, affection shown by soft punch. A light touch to the elbow. See you Monday. Big ships due in. Plenty of work. But the tidal wave of change was on the sea to sweep away this little world. The halfpennies would fall wrong.

Beware.

5

SMOKO

Hairoil O'Reilly ran a budgerigar-breeding business as a front for his after-hours robbery work.

But it was elegant robbery. His work was careful, considered, measured, but most of all it was highly intelligent, for he was highly intelligent. The Dublin word is 'wide'. Nothing to do with education. He was born wide – wide as a wagon of monkeys, as the saying goes.

He had studied the social order and concluded there was nothing at the so-called top that he did not already have. Posh accents and following orders were not for him. Fur coat, no knickers. Losers; sheep: stick it. He was a main man and all who needed to know, knew. No social climbers here.

Every man of standing in the docks kept a loft and raced pigeons. Fanciers – always loved that word. The lofts were kept like little palaces. Each morning the fanciers stood in a line on the bridge which spanned the main shunting yards that led into the port. Height, you see. The pigeons like it. It worked on natural gravity and followed the gentle contour cradling the city to its river. The main lines formed into hundreds of sidings. Each polished track of old silver slithered to the south in the morning sun.

Two ancient steam locos wheezed all day and mothered the trains into their bays, single wagons rolled silently on the grade. At baby-steps speed. Not a sound. Dangerous. Watch your back. Shunters rode the trains by sticking a long paddle into the axles. They sat on them with legs crossed and glided along, easy as pie on the curving tracks. Not a care in the world. Whistling. It looked like a nice way to spend a morning.

The bridge had a wide parapet and fanciers put their cages of birds up on it. Training for racing was serious. This was a 'smoko'. A time of rest, quietness, no sudden moves, soft talk, man to man. This was the birds' time, and they knew it. Flying in joyous, sunlit circles, soaring out over the river and the morning city and back to a helping hand and a warm nest. Then, when the birds had homed, a quiet smoke – a smoko. This was done after signing on at the labour. Mug money, mickey money. Only fools and horses.

Hairoil had followed his father Brylcreem into the exotic-bird business. Yes, it was funny, but you'd laugh behind your hand. They had an Uncle Shiner. No prizes for guessing why. More hair on a goosegog.

Brylcreem had built up a clientele of rich old and not-so-old ladies from the Southside who collected birds. On Sundays, big cars would wait at the top of his terraced street while the ladies viewed his stock. He took them by the side entrance into his shed – his aviary, as he called it. Notions. The wife was at her mother's on Sunday. Refreshment during business was always a Baby Power by the neck as is traditional and proper. He showed them his exotic wares. Say no more. Another satisfied customer.

Every year he sent the wife and her sisters to Benidorm for a fortnight. Respect. This was the social event of the summer for the whole area. His son kept up the family tradition. It was bringing the sisters that gave the trip its power and magic. Tales of moonlight bingo, karaoke by the pool. Jealous whispers. Presents drew a big silent crowd for the unpacking. Once I got a paper sombrero. Heelball, still have it.

Hairoil had a large notebook and binoculars for his bird training.

'What's in the book?' I asked one day.

'There's a front and back,' he said.

'Start at the front,' I said.

'Flying times from France, Holland, Germany ... breeding, training, feeding. We're winners,' he said. 'This is a tough room.'

'And the back?'

'Business,' he said. 'I'll show you. It's in code.' Dense, minute information, rigorous work, cryptic. 'See that line?' he asked. *E.19. x 42. W 4.am.*

'What does it mean?'

'I'll tell you,' he said, 'but you have to take it to the grave, or trouble. Understand?'

'Understood,' I said.

'East, track 19, export, con bogie 42, whiskey, Friday,' he said. 'I know every container. The load every week, every shipping cycle, export/import, every weekly manifest,' he said, looking at the sky. 'I like working out plans, logistical resources.'

'You're wasted,' I said. 'You should be running a large corporation.'

'People like me don't get to run things.'

'How would you get a container out of here?' I asked. 'They must weigh twenty tons.'

'Twenty-three point seven,' he said. 'Did you ever get a puncture? Did you use a jack to lift the car? Did you ever see a big-truck jack? They lift thirty tons. They go under any load. Bottle jacks, they're called.'

'I didn't know that.'

'Listen and learn,' he said. 'Foggy night. *Match of the Day*. Liverpool. Fake roadworks here. Fencing, vans, gear. Four-man team goes down a Jacob's ladder blacked out like the minstrels.'

'Jacob's ladder?'

'Rope ladder with timber steps. Pilots go up them to get onto ships at sea.'

'Right,' I said. 'Simple.'

'Not simple,' he said. 'We don't do simple.'

'What are minstrels?' I asked.

'The Black and White Minstrels. White men blacked up to sing mammy songs. An old TV show still loved around here.'

A favourite story, told and retold. Lino, an old docker watching, said, 'By Jaysus them blacks can sing.'

'Why Lino?' I whispered in Hairoil's ear.

'He's always on the floor.' His brother Rolo was fond of sweets. Easy.

Check container number from my 'notes'. Open front twist locks. Put jacks under corners. Pump. Container will tilt slowly to three feet off bed of rail bogey. Two small strong men get under with silent electric saw. Carefully cut floorboard. Cases of whiskey will come into view. Create human chain. Convey cases to bridge. Lift with mobile electric hoist, twenty cases a lift. Put into vans, leave quietly. Replace floorboards carefully and reseal. Clean whole area spotless. Not a mark. Silence. Total silence.

'Why Liverpool?' I ask.

'People round here think Croke Park is for culchies. It's only up the road. This was an English garrison port. We still do the pools, read English page-three-girl papers, watch soccer. Love Liverpool, love Liverpool. COME ON YE REDS!' he chanted. 'Not a man in that control tower will be sober or take his eyes off the telly during the match. He will shout till hoarse, we would be seen quicker on the moon.'

A pigeon landed. 'That's Mussolini,' he said.

I laughed out loud with delight. The pigeon had the stiff, short legs and self-important strut. He had a puffed-up chest. It was uncanny. All he needed was a row of tiny medals. His malicious eye sought for any imagined slights. Perfect, perfect, perfect.

Months passed. Sitting in Bewley's café skimming the papers. 'Mystery in Yokohama'. Irish container empty on arrival, ship's captain questioned. Seal intact in Dublin, Japanese mafia blamed. Fake seal scam.

The next day I went to the bridge.

'How's Mussolini?' I asked.

'Dead.'

'Jesus.'

'Serves him right,' he said. 'He wasn't winning. Too much showing off. Hawk got him.'

'Yokohama?' I asked.

'The Nips had a good day,' he said. 'I hear they like whiskey.'

I was silent. Poor Mussolini.

'I want to show you something,' he said. He opened the diary at the back, the business end. 'In two weeks, a special load is on its way.'

'What's in it?' I asked.

'Old used notes for incineration.'

'How much would there be,' I said.

'Fifteen million,' he said.

'Fifteen million?' I said.

'Fifteen million,' he said.

There was a long silence.

'I'm looking for a partner,' he said. 'Straight down the middle: 60–40.' No one laughed at the old joke.

'A quiet pint?' he asked. 'Rollicking Biddy's?'

Biddy was a man. Old school tough: no fighting, no biting, no crisps, no credit. Biddy's was a singing house. Strict protocols, Saturday night only. Noble call by Mrs Mac, a lion tamer. Each man, woman, child got a turn. No coaxing. All knew the words and did their best. All got a round of applause and respect. At the end of the night, three songs belted out by the whole house. Crowd-pleasers. And always last, the house favourite: a hurtin' song, a cheatin' song. A woman who wronged her man. Delilah. Who but 'Delilah?' The crowd leaned into the pain, into the hurt. Wishing it away. '*Why, why, why?*' The women knew.

Then: 'Have you no house to go to?' bawled out. The open swallow of the last pint. But no child ever went without new shoes for First Communion if money was tight in a house. Every little girl was asked for a twirl in her new frock. A half-crown each. Any man who beat his wife would feel those iron fists. A man's man. Earrings optional.

Biddy had gone to sea at fifteen, as local men did at the time. Before containers that meant deep sea, blue water. Two years sign on, ship out. He did well. Bosun. Top wages, could lead men. Came home with tidy savings and bought the old pub. Lived upstairs. Had friends but never married. This was quietly accepted: every cripple has his way to crawl.

On a quiet afternoon he would potter behind the bar in a ladies' blouse with a string of pearls, sometimes mascara, always gold earrings and perfume. Never a word said, not a dicky. Your private life is your own. When he did this, sailors showed their tattoos when tattoos were still mysterious. Seamen then could sew, knit, weave, make and mend. Life at sea made them neat and tidy. Shipshape, Bristol fashion. You could see it in them, the way they stood.

Then a ship would be into a foreign port for weeks as cargo was worked by hand from deep between decks by coolie labour. Time to read and write letters. These men were different. They had friends in Japan, Vietnam, Spain. They could set a table properly.

In the snug. Little hatch. Small doors closed. Business being done, men at work. Manners cost nothing. Morning sun outside peeping in as it should be. Two black pints settling nicely, staring up at us. Lovely.

'Well,' he said.

'Here's to Mussolini,' I said. 'Which way does the 60–40 go?'

6

NOT ONLY PIGEONS FLY

Hairoil had been a busy boy. An hour in the morning with his racing pigeons, then a sandwich in the snug of Rollicking Biddy's with Biddy and a small group of men. Fierce, quiet, intense conversation. No notes. No paper. No record. No outsiders. No flash. No mercy. No quarter. To the grave.

Work far into the night. Drive to random distant phone boxes. Never use the same one twice. Driver carries heavy bag of coins.

Away a lot. Travel alone as always. Boat to Liverpool, then who knows. No booking, no name, no ticket, no passport. No record. Anorak, clean jeans, good boots polished. A tidy brickie going to work in England like his father before him. Blend in, head down. Use the loaf, think. Think hard. Every move weighed and measured. Like it says in the book: silence, exile, cunning.

Pre-dawn, winter morning. Mister Sun wonders is there any point in getting out of bed. Foot-stamping time. Mister Frost has done his work. Mister Snow is making up his mind and it's not looking good.

A vast floodlit transport yard, glittering with cold, setting up, ready for the day's work. Heavy diesel engines snorting as they're kicked awake. The slap as tractor units are slammed into trailers. The fifth-wheel mechanism locking the three-inch pin onto the large greased plate. The fifth wheel: that's what makes trucks bendy.

Drivers and yardmen speak quietly beneath staccato bursts of cigarette smoke, blue as blue in the arc lights. 'Queenie, 3.30 pm, Chepstow, on the nose,' into his ear.

Phitchoo, phitchoo, phitchoo. The trailer's air brake chambers fill as the suzies are connected from the cab to the trailer. The bright spirals of red, yellow and blue carry electrics and air to the trailer brakes. Check next time you are beside a big truck in traffic. Now you will know what you are looking at.

Today's job is to load a tanker ship with a million pints of Guinness. Non-haz, strict hygiene, human consumption, twenty-four tons per load. Ten tractor-tankers start at 6 am sharp, finish at noon to catch the tide. Two thousand five hundred tons, sign here please, job done. Except it isn't, not that day. Not that day.

The tanker trailers are slim, polished silver tubes lying at a slight angle. Razzle-dazzle in the sun. Six fat black tyres on silver chrome wheels, Michelin men in blackface. They had been freshly steam-cleaned for the job, and are pure as a young nun. You could eat your dinner off them. Cleaning cert, check. Sealed clean hoses, check. Lights, check. Brakes, check. Fuel, check. Oil and water, check.

Tickety-boo.

Clipboard back on office-wall hook. The ten tractor-tankers lined up down the middle of the yard. Engines running, cabs warm and snug, waiting for barrier to lift. Hold on a mo – message from office. Four government hygiene inspectors will travel today. Snap inspection to check the safety and loading protocols.

Black minivan pulls into yard, four men in white boiler suits get out with briefcases, wearing hygiene masks and baseball hats. The senior man goes into the office and presents his official letter to the yardman.

'Department of the Environment hygiene officer,' he says. 'Shouldn't take more than two hours. You're our star client, best in the business. We won't get in the way, and when we come back we'll bring fig rolls for a nice cup of tea. Do up my report. Sign here please.'

Mrs Kelly in the office, long-married, but still she sees he has a nice bottom in the white boiler suit. It really *is* white. 'When a mummy cares, it shows,' said the old ad before the pictures started.

'All in order, see you soon with the fig rolls.' He gives Mrs Kelly a smile. Ooooooh.

He and his men get into four tractor units. Security barrier lift, trucks move slowly out into the busy morning traffic. Headlights blink hello to mates in trucker code: the rules of the road mean something different down here. They follow the Liffey up to the loading station.

Trucks split up under silos. Still dark, but bright as day in the loading yard. Another blast of steam to ensure clean. The yard inspector breaks the seal, opens the rear valve and signals that loading can commence. A lab technician takes samples in small bottles all along the line.

The government inspectors sit in cabs writing notes and walkie-talkie-ing to each other. They are not friendly, there is no chat. It's official business. 'Sorry, no, I can't tell you where I live, no, I'm not married.' Loose lips sink ships.

A half-hour of six-inch hoses, humping to rhythm, as product is pumped from silo to tankers. Flow gently, Sweet Afton. Automatic cut-off when full. Twenty-four tons exactly. Two men, sideways twist to release valve. Steam hose to clean down connection. Hygiene cover snapped on. Sign here please.

Driver into cab, drives to gate of complex. Gently eases out into the traffic. All ten tankers are now going down the quays to port and spreading out along the route.

Government officials sitting with briefcases on lap. At 8.15 am precisely all cases open, walkie-talkie squawks loud: all four tankers with inspectors are to stop immediately due to an emergency. All four drivers brake hard and stop dead in heavy morning traffic. Immediately, angry horns start blaring.

Government official takes pistol out of briefcase and holds it to driver's head. 'Pull right across all lanes of traffic now or you're a dead man.'

All drivers do as told. Front of tractor units up near Liffey wall with trailer blocking all traffic. Bedlam. Government official takes keys out of ignition and throws into river. He takes heavy steel canister from briefcase and puts on dashboard.

'This is cyanide gas,' he says, 'pre-set release by remote control. I'm getting out now and if you move or open the door it will release and you will die instantly and in agony, as will as all surrounding persons. Give me your phone.'

Throws phone into river.

'Put your hands on wheel.' Handcuffs driver's wrist to wheel. 'Do not touch canister or door for three hours, then you will be safe. Understand? Tell the police not to open the door.'

'Yes I will,' says driver, eyes wide with terror. The government official gets out of the cab. Cuts suzies and hits connectors hard with a hammer. All brakes lock solid. This truck will take hours to move. All four trucks are the same, across all main arterial crossroads.

It takes thirty minutes for the city to come to a stop. People get out of cars to see what's happening. Distant police sirens wail to no avail into the deafening horn-blowing. Tailbacks stretch up the Naas Road and airport road. People lock cars and leave them.

Government officials walk away and melt into crowd.

A separate, empty silver tanker has parked in Dame Street, opposite Trinity and in between the two bank head offices. The driver goes up the inspection ladder and opens all top hatches. He takes four big boom-boxes and puts them on the ground facing in four different directions. He switches them on. He places heavy steel canisters beside them. A huge amplified voice fills the square; a distorted, metallic, foreign accent.

'You are witnessing the biggest bank raid in history. You will not be hurt if you do as we say. Do not approach this area. These canisters contain cyanide. They will activate on movement sensors and many people will die in agony.'

The message keeps repeating, on and on and on and on and on.

The driver unhitches the tractor unit out from the trailer and parks at the Trinity gates. He fires a flare into the cab, which bursts into a huge fireball. Dense black smoke rises into the morning sky. A head appears from the open top hatch of the silver tanker and a man climbs out onto the catwalk. He is followed by seven others. All wear white overalls, hygiene masks, hats and gloves and carry large toolboxes.

They split into two groups and four move to each bank precisely at 10 am as doors open. They walk in with the public. They place large boom-boxes on the counters, switch them on: same message, same voice. Loud. Loud. Very loud. They place six canisters along the counter and order staff to assemble. They ask for the two senior managers to step forward. They tell them the cyanide cylinders are primed to release in forty-five minutes' time: anyone still in the building or within a hundred metres will die instantly.

'I want every safe opened immediately and every safe deposit box opened with the master key. I want your staff to help us load these hundred large canvas sacks. Anyone who does not work will be shot dead.'

In one bank, the manager says, 'I can't do that.'

The official shoots him between the eyes, his head snaps back. Official turns to assistant manager. 'Did you hear my instructions, do you need them repeated? You have ten seconds.'

The assistant manager turns to the assembled staff: 'Open all safes and boxes and help to load sacks immediately, then leave the building when finished. This is an official order.'

The work begins. As each waterproof sack is filled it is carried out of the banks into the street, up the trailer ladder and dropped down hatch into empty tanker. The work is methodical, there is no speaking. The boom-boxes continue their frightening message. The man on the catwalk throws down the sacks from both banks. Not a word, not one single word.

After thirty minutes the tape changes. It says: 'We need to pick up the speed.' The noise reverberates off the building, the staff toil hard and look at their watches. Women sob but work. After forty minutes the boom-boxes stop. Heart-stopping silence over the square. Crowds are moved well back, all sirens off. Quiet as a grave. Bad-tempered seagulls let their annoyance be known.

In both banks, all staff are told to take off their jackets, lie down on their sides and use jackets as pillows. 'It will be over soon,' the boom-box said. Some staff are so stressed they actually fall asleep.

The eight officials walk out to the tankers, take off all gloves, hats, overalls, masks, shoe-covers and place them all in a large pile in the street. One man fires another flare into the pile and the lot goes up with a whoop of flame. Then all eight men lie on the ground, face down, in the total silence of the deserted street, the only noise the crackling of the tractor unit still burning.

Within a minute, the distant *whop whop whop* of heavy rotor blades. Two massive, double-rotor, black military helicopters come up the street at roof height. Ear-crushing noise crashing off buildings. Crowds scatter and run for their lives. First chopper hovers over tanker. Heavy lifting tackle lowered. Man on catwalk closes hatches. He connects tackle to pre-set shackle on top of trailer.

Chopper and trailer rise slowly from the square. Rotor-wash smashing off elegant Georgian façades. Man on catwalk climbs up, lifting tackle and into chopper. Slow banking turn as trailer rises and sails down centre of Westmoreland Street, then turns east downriver and heads to the port and the open sea beyond. Second chopper lowers two ladders and eight men climb up. It too banks away and follows the river to the sea, leaving a deafening silence behind.

Then boom-boxes start again: 'All trailers booby-trapped with cyanide gas, do not approach, all computers and radars in the city have been corrupted and scrambled. Do not enter square for two hours. Repeat, do not enter, do not enter.'

The city sits and waits. At one o'clock an armoured car enters the square. Inside, a four-man army team in gas masks. Public announcements on radio: all car drivers to turn and go home – the city is closed for the day. Streets clear with full curfew. Heavy army presence on street, armoured cars stop and soldiers begin a search. Chatter on radio, 'It's the Russians, the mafia, the I RA, the Latvians.'

Both choppers follow the river to the sea, right down the middle. Silver trailer gleaming in the sun. A hundred feet up. An amazing sight. Crowds stare in silent disbelief. The image is beamed all over the world. Thirty miles out to sea, choppers turn due south. Thirty miles off Wexford coast, silver tanker is lowered gently into the sea. It sinks quietly, no fuss. Choppers turn east and head to an old Soviet submarine base on the Baltic. The sea settles and closes ranks as it always does: the sea can keep a secret.

Twenty-one days later a heavy old Dutch salvage tug shoulders its way up the Irish Sea in a Force Eight gale. Tough as old boots, a bruiser. Registered around the world many times. On survey mission with a crew from every corner of the earth. During the night it holds station in one spot. When the storm passes, four divers go over the side and a heavy lighting rig is lowered down with them. The trailer lies in a hundred feet of water, on its side. Hatches are opened and unloading starts. A hundred heavy waterproof sacks come to the surface. A winch is lowered and the bags are brought up, four at a time.

As dawn breaks, the job is finished and the tug heads east to the Baltic. One week later, as per contract, each member of a twenty-man military team receives €1 million into a numbered bank account. No names, no pack drill. They never meet or speak again.

The government announced that security had not been breached: a lie. The government says the robbers got away with €30 million: another lie, it was multiples of that. The diamonds, gold and bonds did not surface on the black market for years. What was in the safe-deposit boxes will never be known. The police said they were following a definite line of inquiry: another lie.

Hairoil and his fellow fanciers watched the trailer flying down the Liffey while they trained their pigeons. They took pictures of it with them all firmly in the frame, in that place, at that time. Later, in the snug of Rollicking Biddy's, Hairoil allowed himself one joke. Not only pigeons fly.

7

RUSTLING AT
UNDERNOSE FARM

Hairoil burnt his notes. Carefully, one page at a time. He crumbled the ashes into a glass of slops. Torn-up notes could be put back together. Prying eyes. Not good. Could all end in tears. Secrets are secret. The rest is silence.

Sitting in his head office, the snug of Rollicking Biddy's. The owner, Biddy, his lifelong friend and mine, a sailor home from the sea. 'Do not disturb' in Hairoil's eyes. Men at work.

He was reviewing his vast criminal business. New direction, endgame. Quiet, fierce intelligence, concentration, line by line, man by man, deal by deal. Shaking out weaknesses, testing the machine, probing, sifting, smelling the air, settling scores. Two men would die. Business is business, it would be soon. Calls made. Same routine, randomly chosen public payphones, no mobiles, no computers, no paper, no strangers, cash, dirty cash, long, long chain of command. Please do not touch the goods.

He sat back and took a break. Looked forward to tomorrow's treat. Once a month he and Biddy took two lines of the finest, purest cocaine. Never more, never less.

They went to the zoo, as always. In a battered old van, ex-P&T, bright orange, quiet laugh. To see their old friend Charlie, Cheeky Charlie. Charlie knew them well. They loved him dearly. He had a tyre hanging from a rope. He looped one arm into the tyre like a man leaning on a bar counter. Relaxed like. He crossed his legs down low at the ankles. He looked them in the eye, fair and square. *How are things in Glocca Morra?* he seemed to say. *Turned out nice.* A steady, strong, manly gaze. Not a bother on him. A man's man. One of our own. A pal.

Then the drum-roll moment. Biddy lit a cigarette – Charlie liked Rothman's – and handed it to him through the bars. Charlie took the fag daintily. Quick look to ensure it was properly lit. Took a slow, reflective drag, the cigarette held at the edge of his big dry lips. Eyes half closed. A shiver of pleasure passed among the group. Then the best. He cupped the cigarette in his hand and nonchalantly put it behind his back and resumed his gaze. Not piercing, but searching, open, honest, assured, respectful. They had taught him to do this years ago, as they used to do when they were boys, with a gang of pals, standing at street corners. 'Charles', as it said on the sign on the cage, placed the cigarette on his thumb and with two fingers flicked it back to them. Like all the best laughs in school, they could not laugh out loud. It would be rude, might cause offence. Inside, they screamed. Charles demanded and got respect and, from his point of view, the courtly and formal ritual of a friend's visit had been observed with dignity and style. All in order. No need for bananas. The whole ape enclosure was paid for by a benevolent fund in Jersey. The guard went for his tea when he saw them, if you follow my drift. The funds were from a Bahama lawyer's office with nominee directors. Say no more.

On to an old country pub on the banks of the Liffey. Sitting out in the little yard over the river, settled in nicely.

'Two nice pints, please, and two sausage sandwiches.'

'Certainly,' said the old lady who ran the pub. 'Lovely to see you again.'

'You're looking well,' Hairoil said. 'I hear you're getting engaged.'

'You're an awful man,' she said. 'Who'd have me?'

'I hear you're a snug woman with twenty-five grand in the post office. I'd say you are a catch, and great legs too. I might have an interest myself.'

'The last time I saw twenty-five was on a bus,' she said. 'I had a young man once, I loved him beyond reason and into madness. He went to their stupid war and never came back. I could never look at another.' The pale morning light trembled with her sadness.

She went to make the sandwiches. Silence tiptoed. The river moved on. The drugs coursed their golden magic. They sat together as happy as a man could be. Blissful.

'Lucky men,' Hairoil said.

'Lucky men,' Biddy said.

A gentle elbow in the ribs. A chuckle.

The old lady came back with a tray. Lovely creamy pints, fresh batch bread, four fat sausages smiling.

'Heaven,' said Biddy. 'Where would you get it?'

'Put a horn on a corpse,' Hairoil said.

Old, long-practised patter, a little word-canter. Old friends at ease. It continued.

'Are you a mustard man, yourself?' Biddy asked.

'Ah no, the mammy had me ruined with the red ketchup. "Get it into you son," she said. I told her, "You're a desperate woman."'

He bit into his sandwich. The taste exploded and soared in his mouth, while the pure cocaine drove pulsing delight to every fibre of his body. The old lady felt the silence and the slow chewing of her strange customers and went back to the shadows of her little kitchen. Her lost young lover stood beside her. She cried where they could not see her, her tears running over her old hands. She cursed God and damned her soul.

She would never know that the younger man out in the yard owned the pub and had been looking after her for years. She was told that the rent freeze was due to a legal issue over title. Not her problem, her solicitor said, say nothing. She said nothing. The law is an ass.

They gave her a big tip and told her they had done well on a job as small builders. They said they would be back soon, for a child's big communion party, take over the place for the day.

'Keep a dance for me,' said Hairoil.

'You're too kind,' she said. 'Your van looks banjaxed. I hope if we get married, you'll do better than that.'

'My other car is a Jaguar,' said Hairoil. 'I will strew your path with rose petals on the way to our nuptial couch. We will lie as one among the stars.'

'Are you sure you don't need anything before we go?' he asked. 'You know we love your place. I might propose to you next time, so stay away from handsome men till I get back.'

They both saw her red eyes, and knew. She waved to them all the way up the winding river road as they drove away in their little orange van.

Men, what are they like? she asked herself.

. . . .

Strange days indeed. I was standing at the gate of our yard when a young boy spun around on his new chopper.

'Hey, mister, Stab the Rasher wants to see you in Biddy's,' he said. 'Quiet pint.'

'Cheeky pup,' I said, 'Tell him I'll be round in an hour.'

'Tell him yourself, big shot. Where's my tip?'

I had known Hairoil all my life, but I was never seen with him. I got a turkey at Christmas with no note. I nodded to him when we met.

I went to Biddy's, into the snug. Hairoil and Biddy were waiting. No drinks. A small screen open in front of them. Sunlight fell on rows of sparking glasses.

'Our relationship is about to change,' he said. 'I have tracked you for many years.'

'I greatly admire you and your work. It would be an ambition one day to be your partner in a new life,' he said.

The pub was empty, a woman sweeping. Everything spotless. I said nothing.

'I want to show you this,' he said.

He flicked the screen. It showed a group of wild young boys racing sulky ponies flat out along a busy motorway, heavy traffic backed up behind. It had become a notorious image when talking heads on TV spoke of the breakdown of society. Spread out across the lines of traffic, the long whips singing out to frenzied ponies pulling lightweight chariots with bicycle wheels. It caused a sensation. A big country sergeant waffled on the telly. Outrage, etc. Nothing happened. Funny that.

'Some of those ponies where mine,' Hairoil said. 'Stolen from my farm. Stolen from me.'

'You have a farm?' I said. 'Where is it?'

'That's what I want to talk to you about,' he said. Nothing would surprise me, but I was wrong.

'I want to bring you for a little drive,' he said.

The three of us walked out and got into one of his many vans. This one read 'Maureen: Wedding Dresses,

Home Fittings, Satisfaction Guaranteed for the Fuller Figure, Paris-trained'. Droll. Our boy was always droll.

We drove to his shed behind our main yard. The policeman on the corner carefully studied the house opposite.

Into the shed. Like all his places, it was spotless. A row of vans. Plumbers, roofers, hearing aids, a few good, plain cars, nothing flash. Never flash. A door at the back. Steep stone steps down. Another door. Chilly. Opened into a new world.

A beautifully built vaulted ceiling, good brick, Dolphin's Barn Dublin brick. A 200ft-long curved roof, fully lit, above row after row after row of cages containing every type of bird. Budgies, singing birds, parrots, linnets. I was in shock.

'My party piece,' he said, 'in honour of my father, a well-known bird man. He was fond of you.'

He slid back the little curtain on a big cage. An old parrot blinked into the light. Hairoil rang his nail along the bars and whistled softly.

'Two pints of larger and a packet of crisps please,' said the parrot. 'How's your belly for a lodger, missus?' Then a cackle. Haroil gave the bird a peanut and slowly closed the curtain. Show over. Short and sweet. Call my agent.

'I've been trying to tell you for years,' he said. 'There's more.' Boy, was there more. We walked to the back wall. A large hole had been opened in the Victorian brickwork. I stepped through and into another world. It sounds corny, but I could not believe my own eyes.

Three huge vaulted caverns stretched away into the distance, directly under our yard, each lined with white-painted pens and a central walkway. Looped cable carried bare bulbs. Sheep, goats, ponies, dogs and litters of pups, hens, turkeys, grazing and feeding peacefully. A full working farm, right under the city. Overhead, a modern air-handling system pumped fresh air. Everything clean and proper, as always with Hairoil. He saw me looking up.

'I took it from a computer factory I bought,' he said. From him, that could mean anything.

We walked slowly down through the farm to the end wall, passing by livestock, hay bales, men sweeping.

I heard a noise, growing louder. Now I could not believe my ears. It was the propellers of a ship mooring outside. We were just below the river. Like in a submarine movie, every sound carried in the water.

I gazed at the wall in amazement. When I looked down, a goat was carefully nibbling my hat where I held it in my hand. The ship reversed her screws so that the noise was deafening as she came alongside.

When the noise died away, Hairoil said: 'I love the madness of it. I found it years ago when I was searching for a leak in the floor of my father's budgie business. It started out as a joke, it just grew. Part of the fun was that you did not know, never mind the culchie cop outside. I knew you would like it. You and me.'

'We can't be partners,' I said, 'You're a crim and I'm a five eight.'

'I'm going to be a five,' he said. 'I've sold my international drug operation. My raiding team is disbanded and paid off. Rich man every one. Pensions. There are new days coming. The new rock venue down the road will bring many new people down here didn't know our world existed. The millions of shares I bought for pennies in early tech companies years ago bring in more money that I can spend in a hundred lives. There's no point in robbing. It's all clean now. We should go into the property business, you and me. Open up the docks. Partners, straight down the middle, 60–40. Old joke, I couldn't resist.

'I can't control the young guys anymore,' he went on. 'The smartest ones know the world is loaded against them, with their accents and this address. Even if they do go to school, they'll only end up in front of a screen in a faceless open office with hundreds of other mugs. Drive an hour and a half to a cheap crappy house in an estate with a fake name. To spend their lives paying a mortgage. They know the bullshit guff words, *mission statement, customer service, team-building, Q4,* guff to make gobshites feel important. It's a con job. No way José, the real winner sits by a pool in California reading philosophy and shooting grouse in Scotland in season before wintering in the south of France. "Nice bit of tweed, my lord." They carry guns. They're not afraid. They know the score. My day is done. The fives will win because they rob honestly.'

'You cannot carry on now that I've seen this,' I said. 'I know.'

'Open it to the public,' I said, 'it would be a tourist magnet. A gold mine.'

'You don't get it,' he said. 'It was never about money. It was for you. It's the madness of it. That would be gone. It would be Disney. Americans in yellow trousers looking for the T-shirt shop. "Have you any leprechauns?" I'll close it down, I need six months.'

'No drugs, no stolen goods on the premises,' I said.

'My word,' he said.

'That'll do,' I said.

'Will you be my partner in the new world coming down here?' he asked. 'Clean as a whistle.'

'No,' I said. That *no* cost me uncountable millions.

They asked me back to Biddy's for a pint. I said no.

Six months later to the day, as promised, three of us stood in the middle of our main yard. A fifty-ton road-breaker punched into the ground with a shuddering *rat-a-tat-tat*. A huge hole appeared. The machine was stopped. We all stood around the hole and looked down into that beautiful model farm, all pens swept out and empty, row after row. The first light of heaven in a hundred and fifty years poured down on this bizarre and beautiful work of art. One man took out his phone.

'Take a photo and I'll break both your legs,' Hairoil said. 'It was built after the Famine by the Protestants to feed the poor. It was called Undernose Farm. The health and safety man wants it closed.' They did not get the joke, but I did.

'That's funny,' I said. 'Undernose Farm, that's funny.'

It took six days to fill it up with gravel and rubble. We had destroyed a masterpiece. I never got a bill.

One year later I was stuck in traffic. A black limo stopped outside the new twenty-storey Bank of Arabia. My man got out. Pinstriped suit, snowy-white shirt, pink tie, dainty pumps, the works. A beautiful blonde PA carried papers. He clocked me, walked over to my car.

'Undernose Holdings have already bought fifteen large sites along the river. They have doubled in value already. The banks are raining money down on me. Come to Saudi with me tomorrow. Change your mind. I tell all my new friends I have known you all my life. They are impressed. You have the magic dust I will never have. People like you, they don't like me. They fear me. Come to Saudi, they are sending a private jet.'

The policeman on the corner gave a little salute and a smile. Hairoil and I looked at each other. The wolf was in the fold. Christ in heaven help them.

'I will put something special in the turkey this year,' he said. You'll never guess what it was.

Weeks later, I went to the zoo. I was first in. I went straight to Charlie's cage, or should I say Charles'. He was sitting against the back wall, legs stretched out. He seemed to have aged. Do gorillas look old or young? He did not know me. He yawned, a huge yawn. We looked at each other for half an hour, in silence. I felt like saying, Hairoil and Biddy send their regards.

To me he was a slightly puzzled old man who had gone for a little doze and woken up to a changed world. I know the feeling. I had brought a banana. When he saw it he came to me with his Teddy-boy shuffle, shoulders held high. He peeled it slowly and ate it with relish, but nicely. He politely handed me back the skin and held his ground.

But I had a plan.

Thank you, Charles. I will name my new company after you, Charles Holdings Ltd. You will be the richest gorilla in Dublin. No, not a pinstripe. Perhaps a dressy dark blue. Classy. But pink? Never. Never. I'm a pinstripes man. Charles nodded his approval. We would look after business, Charles and I.

8

WIDOWS' MEMORIES

Allow me to introduce my gang of four. A fine body of men. First up, The Little Flower, a good scrapper. Fears no man. Age: fourteen years. The Prof, yes, you got there before me: thick as plaited pig shit. But sometimes he said things that swayed and shimmered in the air and brought a silence. Then Skin: more meat on a butcher's pencil. Courage of a lion. Age: fourteen years. Snag: smart, smart and cunning, a good planner, our second-in-command. Officer material. Age: fifteen-and-a-half years. Then there's yours truly. Leader. El Supremo. A looker. All-round good egg. Age: fourteen-and-a-half years.

We were meeting in central HQ, a huge old 1950s American Chevrolet dumped at the bottom of my dad's yard. Overgrown with nettles. Good camouflage in the event of surprise attack. Deep leather back seat, squeaky springs. Lovely old smell on a sunny day. My uncle Joe, with the club foot, known to one and all as Hopalong, ran it as a taxi during the war. I used to try on his special boot. Nice. A rich American woman once gave him a £25 tip. Fond of the ladies, our Joe. A charmer. Runs in the family.

Our meeting was held with us all piled on top of each other on the big back seat. Boys like this. It's called a scrag. There was plenty of room in the front but it was never used. It was for guests only, our good room, mind the ornaments.

The yard and our Chevrolet hideout was on the riverfront at the old port. It was surrounded by stacked cargo and trailers, facing south, a sun trap.

One famous day the gang were in among the nettles on a carpet, an old Persian rug from my granny's good room, taking the air. There was a high spring tide and the river was nearly up to the top of the wall. Fast-ebbing, swollen, dangerous.

Suddenly a seal. Curved scimitar back as they do, a crescent moon. Floating on his back, relaxed as a deckchair. Half-eaten salmon under his flipper. Lunch. He saw us as we saw him. Twelve eyes locked in a primal stare. His gaze told of mild interest, gentle and slightly puzzled. He sailed swiftly past on the tide, his fish forgotten. He was our friend from that moment, our guiding star. The Day of the Seal. Don't worry. Be happy.

It was a slack day. Short agenda. We were on a comic-reading break. Sharing a borrowed Woodbine. Three drags per man, don't Bogart the joint.

Then Prof said one of his things. 'Why don't we save up and plan a big day out? Do all our favourite outings and finish with a blowout?' Altogether, comics down, pondering, nodding, murmurs of approval, lips moving in calculations.

I immediately took command. I know my men.

'How much are we talking here,' I asked.

'Two-and-six per man,' he said. This has to be money no object. The world's our lobster.

Snap-decision time. 'Let's do it,' I said. Leader. El Supremo.

The meeting came to life. All ideas were put forward. Serious stuff. Debating, yes, no, maybe. One idea: we would go to the Spanish gypsy woman who worked at the corner of Misery Hill. Fierce row, idea was shot down. We were too young. She was old, some said nearly thirty. She'd take all our money. She was a bit frightening. She could only pick one of us to be her 'companion'. She had a sister, bit of a dog. Trap six, Harold's Cross. But what about the others? Equality, as the Frogs say, one for all.

Finally, a day's programme of events emerged. It was unanimous.

1. Bus stop 9 am sharp.
2. Pool money in the special sock. I would be bag man, of course.
3. Bring chocolate. You're not you when you're hungry.
4. Visit our old friends the shrunken heads.
5. Shake the hand of the Dead Nun.
6. Go to penny dinners. Blag in. Discuss tactics.

7. Visit 100-ton crane. Review plan for entry.

8. Broadway caff. Blowout. Tightener.

And so it came to pass the following Saturday.

On bus, as usual pay three fares: the other two are 'special needs'. Good acting. Practice makes perfect. One woman makes the sign of the cross. 'Their poor mother,' she says. All piled into one seat. Good scrag.

Into the museum. Celtic crosses, boring. Early manuscripts, boring. Chalices, boring. History stuff, boring. Third floor, glass case at the back. Our three pals. Lovely. They smile when they see us, their little orange faces the size of a child's fist. Twinkly eyes that follow you round the room. Long black shiny hair like John Rocha. They look in good humour, even cheerful in difficult circumstances. A little smile as we leave. They know – they just know – that they are much loved. 'See you next Tuesday,' to the guard.

Read instructions on how they are made. First catch a person you don't like. Behead. Cut the top of skull off. Empty contents. Fill with hot stones. Lovely. Keep up the hot-stones process over three months. Hang in smoky tent for twelve months. Love it. Life today is dull. Beheading frowned upon. No hot stones. Wash your hands. Nicely nice. No wonder crime has soared. Bring back beheading, I say.

Back on the street. Next up St Michan's. Walk along quays to Four Courts. Crowds of Americans out in front. Tourists are a nuisance. They should be banned. In and down the clammy steps. Sudden cold and dark.

Torch waving at end of long black corridor.

'Don't step on a coffin,' says the torch.

'What, in these shoes?' I say, an old line, I know.

Echoes, intense cold, not good. You don't want to be a big girl's blouse down here.

Heavy, rusted-steel gate. One weak bulb. Coffins propped against wall. Lids thrown back. One long brown leather person. Looks like sleeping off fourteen pints. Bad pints. Next, a midget leather thing. The nun. Outstretched shiny, tiny hand. Polished, long black dirty nails, claws like a rat's. Suggestive leer from ear to ear, except there are no ears. As leader, I put my hand in first. I looked into the vacant sockets. Fear. Each man in turn then flees to the little square of blessed sunlight splashed on the cruel stone floor.

Out to the light, the surge of being alive jumped from body to body. Next up, lunch. The tricky one. The penny dinners. To blag in was a badge of honour. Meet the expert. Five gold medals.

Back down the quays. Quiet outside. People carrying cheap bags containing their lives. Big nun with headdress of high white wings controlling the door. I mean, really big. Frau Obergruppenführer. Our well-oiled plan springs into action. Four men up lane to hide.

I stand at back of queue, slightly out to side. Snivelling. Quiet sobbing muffled in dirty hankie.

Frau O comes down the queue. 'What's wrong with you?' she asks.

'Nothing,' I say.

'What's your name?'

'Kevin,' I say. No it isn't.

'Tell me what's wrong.' She leans down. She has a five o'clock shadow like Desperate Dan. 'Step over here,' she says. 'Whisper.' Stubble at mill.

'My da came home drunk and smashed up the house. He threw our dinner out into the street. He beat my ma with a chair. He put his fist through the telly and it's not even paid for. Me and my brothers ran for our lives. We slept under the canal bridge.'

'When did you last eat?' she asks.

'Thursday,' I say. 'We found a loaf under a Bewley's van.' I made that up on the spot. Raw talent. I'm wasted.

'Have you any money?'

'No,' I say, 'but I could give you my miraculous medal. One of my brothers has a penny. He could go in and bring a bit out for us.' All this blinded with tears.

'Get your brothers and follow me.' I like firmness in a woman.

In like Flynn. Sorted. Still bawling, huge hiccups. You can't fake a hiccup. Ask anyone.

Five of us at a long factory table. Then pure magic. Each knife and fork hanging on a little chain. Pilfer-proof. Brillo. I vowed that when I'm rich and famous I will have gold chains on my knives and forks. In a castle.

Queue. Four heavy steel bowls of steaming stew. Two lumps of bread. Margarine. Get it inti ya, Cynthia.

At the other end of our table, two tramps. Not a tooth between them. Arms around their stew and bread. Who's going to rob your stew when you 'can get it free up there?'

'Bugger off,' one tramp says. 'Cheeky pup.'

'What did you do with your teeth?' I ask him.

'I gave them to a Jap for a loaf of bread on the death railway in Burma.'

Was it sliced pan? I was going to say, but maybe in poor taste. I did not.

Sister Stubble panzered down the aisle. 'Have you stopped crying?' she asks.

'Have you any chips?' The Little Flower asks. She ignores him.

'All down on your knees for the Rosary,' she says, Desperate-Dan chin out.

'We will first go to the boys' room,' I say. A jiffy. Into toilet. One small window open. Polished team effort. Out the window and away like shit off a shovel. Rosary, my arse. There's no such thing as a free lunch. You'd want to be up all night, even the nuns pushing something. I ask you. Is nothing sacred?

Last item, 100-ton crane. Renew our plan to conquer it. At dock gate tell man our mothers sent us here to get money from our das before they went to the pub. In. Stand at legs of giant crane. Old, rusty, dignified, beautiful as an old lady can be. Gate closed with big chain and padlock, keep out. Bill Brown is the only man allowed to the top. You can see Wales from there. The magic was this: he told a hushed crowd one morning that he saw women playing tennis in Holyhead in little white frocks. Clear as day in the early morning light, in Wales. Wales. Never mind the U-boat during the war.

This would be our next outing. Bill drank with my father. Our plan, like all good plans, simple. Take his keys from overcoat when he was drunk in our house. Press into bar of soap like in the movies. Cut copy. Climb crane at dawn to wait for tennis and see women. Easy. One day.

Our work done, the Broadway Café. Bright lights, big city. I remembered my da had given me a note for when I got there. I opened it. It was a good note: a pound note. Geddit? Talk about excitement.

Call over waitress. The beautiful one. Tight red uniform, big smile, red lips. I fall in love as she walks over. Head over heels. My fifth time in love, I knew the score. Love hurts. She has a little white pad, a lovely little white pad.

'What's your favourite band?' I ask.

'None of your business, you cheeky pup.'

Opening gambit. There are many moves in life's chess game. 'Resistance is futile,' I say. 'Destiny calls.' Churchill, my hero, said that.

'Order or out,' she says. A fighter.

'Four sausage and chips with extra chips. Then four Knickerbocker Glories.'

'What colour jelly?' she asks, looking round the table.

Red. Red. Red. Green. There's always one.

Food comes. Like feeding the lions at the zoo. My uncle calls sausages 'widows' memories'. Quiet snigger. I go up to pay. Give her a sixpenny tip.

'Be patient,' she says, 'your time will come.'

'I was only showing off in front of my mates.'

'I know,' she says, and smiles and touches my hand. 'Wait. Just wait.'

As I said, love hurts.

Next morning debriefing at hideout. Snag did not show. Funny, that. Or the next day. Or the next.

Friday night sitting outside chipper. On our bench. Large singles. Mrs Fusco was famous for her one joke, delivered deadpan.

'Will the chips be long?' from the queue.

'About three inches.' Always funny.

Snag showed up and sat down. No hello. 'I'm out of the gang,' he said. I dropped my chips. 'I went to see the Spanish gypsy woman on my own.' Shocked silence. Chips on the ground cooling. 'I went twice,' he said. 'And we're going to the pictures.'

'Did you? ... Are you?' I stammered.

'Yes,' he said.

On that bench, on that night, at that hour, our boyhood ended, our gang broke up. Never saw him again. Word was he went to Spain with his lady. I hope he finds happiness. It's elusive. We all need to give it our best shot. Never did see the ladies in Wales. Pity.

9

SURE, A BIRD NEVER
FLEW ON ONE WING

'Bastard. Miserable, mean, selfish bastard,' a docker said to his mates as the excise officer passed by in his shiny Ford Anglia. Many heads nodded in agreement.

The car was his pride and joy. You know the type. Hand-cut, flowered house carpet on the inside floor and in the boot. Plastic flowers on dash. Extra wing mirrors. Special chrome hubcaps. He took the wife out on Sunday for a drive and parked at Dollymount strand reading the papers with the windows closed. Fresh air. They wore their slippers and cardigans, which they kept in the car for the purpose. Bastard.

A plot was hatched. Revenge is sweet. During a quiet lunch hour when he was up at head office a forklift expertly lifted the car and carried it to a container compound. Hundreds of eyes watched in cunning silence. It was lowered in front of an empty container with the doors open. Many willing hands pushed it through the doors, which were then slammed shut and locked. The container was bound for Bombay, stowed as deck cargo on a five-week winter passage across the Indian Ocean. The car vanished. Gone, never to be seen again. It was not tied down or secured in any way. The ship hit a typhoon. The slippers were the only thing not smashed into a small metal tangle.

The excise officer worked with his assistant, known as a producer, and a carpenter in a special high-security warehouse, which housed only expensive brandies, vintage wines, whiskeys, liqueurs. Their job was to tap sample kegs to check alcohol content for duty.

The carpenter used a heavy wooden mallet and chisel to open old casks. The producer inserted a long clear glass tube open at both ends. He dipped the tube into the cask and placed his thumb over one end. When he lifted out the tube it showed a sample. This was emptied into a glass phial by removing his thumb so that the liquid flowed. The excise officer then put the government-calibrated hydrometer onto the surface of the liquid where it floated at a depth dependent on the alcohol content. This was read off the side markings and entered into the log. The duty could then be assessed.

The sample was known as 'the angels' share' and traditionally the samples were shared out at the end of the day with a taste for all working on the ship. The officer changed all this. He put the samples into bottles and brought them home. Not a good idea.

There were also many gifts of expensive wines and spirits from grateful shippers and agents. Again, not shared. Again, not good.

Another plot was hatched. A strange piece of cargo arrived one day on a French shallow-sea vessel, an ancient brandy cask lying on its side and expertly roped onto a pallet. It was clearly marked as 'Nelson Trafalgar Brandy' and addressed to Professor Roland Lindon, Trinity College, Dublin. It was heavily sealed and embossed with red wax stamps. 'Sorbonne, Paris', it said. 'Do Not Disturb. Do Not Use'. An old docker removed this sign. Quiet laughing echoed around the nearly empty ship's hold.

The old cask swung out over the river as it came up out of the hatch and into daylight. It was carried by forklift into the excise store. There were many conflicting opinions among the dockers as to what it was. All experts to a man, of course. The received wisdom that this must be the finest and oldest brandy in the world, seeing as how it was being given to Trinity College by the Sorbonne, no less.

It lay in the cool dark warehouse for a few days while the excise man controlled his curiosity and worked out exactly what he would say in his report. He looked forward to sharing the angels' share with his friends rather than with coarse dockers who did not possess a palate subtle enough to appreciate such a renowned and rare vintage.

Next morning the three-man team set to work. The heavy red wax seal of the Sorbonne was gently removed, and the bung carefully opened. A rich, powerful aroma filled the air. Knowing glances were exchanged.

'Must be a hundred years old,' said the carpenter. 'The big shots and toffs in Trinity will enjoy this after their feast.'

The glass tube went in. The thumb was applied. The tube was extracted full of a dark, golden liquid. The thumb was removed and the precious fluid flowed into a glass phial. The cask was resealed with an Irish Customs Bond marker. Next day it was delivered to the professor in Trinity.

Word filtered back that the excise man and his wife and friends all agreed it was a life-enhancing experience to be allowed to taste this piece of history. The excise man's wife had a second small snifter. 'Sure, a bird never flew on one wing,' she said, laughing.

One week later two pieces of mail arrived at the excise office. A small parcel containing two pairs of slippers, one ladies', one gents', both badly torn by flying glass. Also a badge from a Ford Anglia. Attached to the letter was a photo of a small ball of metal sitting on Mumbai docks surrounded by a crowd of bystanders dressed in white robes for the intense heat. The letter said: *Sahib, it is with a broken heart and many griefs I send you metal of fine car much broken on the sea. With God's will the much unlucky owner will survive heavy sads and have many sons.*

The other was a letter from the medical faculty at Trinity College. Its tone was curt and ominous:

Sir, we are at a loss to understand why our recent shipment was interfered with. It was clearly marked 'not for consumption'. When Nelson was killed at Trafalgar, the defeated French gave a cask of finest brandy so that the body of the fallen warrior could be sent home tied to the mast of HMS *Victory to be buried in Westminster Abbey.*

To celebrate the historic joining together of our medical teaching faculties, the Sorbonne sent us a cask of brandy containing severed heads, legs, arms, fingers, eyes, ears and brains, all samples with diseases for study including cancer, syphilis, leprosy, plague and pox. All were in advanced stages of decomposition.

Should any of this material have fallen on clothes of workers or touched their hands, we advise an immediate and full medical examination. Please do not interfere with our goods in future. The Minister has been informed of our displeasure.

Signed: Professor Roland Lindon, Medical Faculty, Trinity College.

The excise officer did not have a good day.

10

GIVE US BARABBAS

Before containers, loose cargo came in cartons, packing cases, timber boxes, pallets, and often went 'slack', which meant broken.

Contents were visible and had to be stabilized so that at least the packaging was delivered for insurance count. It was signed off as STC ('said to contain') 100 dolls, say. You can imagine the rest.

The crews of ships also conducted a steady trade in goods that went in and out of fashion. Polish ships cornered the market one year in brightly checked lumber-jack shirts. Large numbers of dockers, young and old, turned up for work looking like American folk singers, or student protesters. Another year, Chinese ships brought a flood of Chairman Mao blue padded work jackets, with toggles, as on a duffel coat. I wore one for years. They are now the height of fashion with trendy Southside social revolutionaries who have nothing and want to share it.

Barabbas drove a seven-ton forklift. He was a born hustler, or gifted capitalist entrepreneur, depending on how you see the world. His forklift had many gear storage areas, toolboxes, secret places. All of these where stuffed with a wide selection of goods to suit every taste. Bang on trend, bang on price. He conducted a thriving business as he drove around the docks visiting his loyal client base. They came to him for wedding and anniversary gifts and Holy Communion presents.

If he hadn't got in stock the item a customer wanted, he would take an order for it. That meant a gentle nudge of the rear of his forklift to the corner of a packing case as he passed by on his duties. 'Slack': are you still with me? Having made the necessary adjustment to the packaging, he didn't even bother to get off the forklift, but drove on. His hands never left his wrists, oh no, our boy was too wide for that.

During a pilferage clampdown, Barabbas was called to head office. Serious. He told the manager he was shocked and disappointed to be told that pilferage was happening in his workplace. He was ever vigilant and would immediately write a report if any incident happened while he was working a ship. He would name names. Show no mercy, as was only right and proper.

He was asked if he had ever pilfered. He said that last year he had eaten a bar when he was helping to tape up a broken pallet of chocolate. Fruit and nut. It had been on his conscience ever since. He had lit a candle to St Anthony, the patron saint of those who had fallen into sin. The manager sat in stony silence, and wrote down Barabbas's confession.

When word got out that Barabbas had been brought to the office, hundreds of dockers in between decks of several deep-sea ships started a chant:

'Give us Barabbas!'

'Give us Barabbas!'

'Give us Barabbas!'

It was meant to be funny but the voices of hundreds of unseen men coming up from open hatches to join their voices to the chant made for a strange and haunting scene, one that men would never forget.

Barabbas became a star turn in local pubs, being called on over and over to tell his story of the bar of chocolate and the candle to St Anthony.

On the last Friday before Christmas, after work at 5 pm sharp, he arranged his annual fashion and accessory show for his clients in the pub beside the Point Depot. This was the social highlight of the year – standing room only. Foreign seamen were welcome.

A small, bald docker named Jem became Jemima for the evening, and sashayed up and down before the crowd, modelling a selection of ladies' frocks, coats, handbags. 'Slack'. He got tumultuous applause, wolf whistles, offers of marriage, lewd suggestions; he was even pinched on the bottom. Barabbas gave a running commentary of fashion trends re colour, sleeve length, hem height, mix and match. He also set out in some detail the various outcomes when a grateful wife or girlfriend got her new frock, coat or handbag. Jemima, ever demure and in a ladylike fashion supported these few words with a small, tasteful mime, which left no doubt as to a positive conclusion. The packed pub roared their approval.

All items were sold 'off the model' as the show progressed. Jemima dressed and undressed for the client on the spot. Trade was cash only, no haggling allowed. Barabbas put all proceeds behind the bar for free drink for all. Sailors brought Polish vodka, Chinese brandy, blue and red liqueurs with names in strange script.

Each year there was a special surprise treat. One time, everyone in the audience got a huge bar of Toblerone, another year, expensive sunglasses. Jemima got her handbag filled from a grateful and adoring audience. The evening usually ended with arm-wrestling and the singing of cowboy songs.

In the new year Jem was promoted to 'singer out'. This meant standing on a platform on deck looking down into the open hatch and guiding the crane driver who could not see down into the bottom of the ship. The singers out used a rolled-up newspaper for better visibility. It was an important skill and brought safety to those working below, 'under the hook'. It was a little bit of theatre: the singers out were stars.

One day the wind swung a heavy hoist of timber the wrong way. It knocked Jem off balance, and he fell through the safety rail and down through all the decks to the bottom of the ship.

All work was stopped that day. His broken body, resting on a blood-soaked sheet, was lifted out on a pallet by crane for all to see. Men wept. Jem had been much loved. His huge funeral stopped all traffic, and went on for days.

The Barabbas fashion show never took place again. The magic was gone. When Barabbas saw his first container, he resigned. He opened a chain of shops and became a millionaire.

His fashion business offerings are now a must-have for the glitterati at the top of society. His brand name is 'Jemima', as it should be. Little do his customers know. 'The past is another country,' as the man said.

11

RATTLE

Vantastic. No. *Van Ordinaire.* No. *One Boy One Van.* No. *Boy Meets Van.* No.

I was going into the removals business. I needed a catchy name. I believe in starting at the top. School finished, beginning of summer. I needed work, I needed money. Serious money.

At seventeen, a motorbike, three girlfriends, drink, fags, party every night – it mounts up. My financial standing would not suit Mr Micawber. My father said I could use one of his small vans to look for work at the weekend. Perfect. Cut out interviews. Suited me grand, as I am crippled with shyness and crushed self-esteem. I am not a natural employee. I see myself as management.

In those days, antique dealers put their furniture outside their shops on Saturday mornings. Georgian furniture was cheap, there was no shortage. Big houses were selling up all over Ireland.

I printed my first flyer: *Across the street, around the world.* Modest, understated, my style. It set a tone, I thought. Another one: *We will do anything for a fiver.* Not classy, too needy, a bit clingy. And: *Let us handle your drawers* (snigger). No, of course we did not use that one. Well, O K, a few times in the Bailey, my new office. Mixed results.

Saturday morning, sunny. An old Georgian Dublin street. Shops open, gear outside, lined up. People, mostly women, middle-class women, viewing. My assistant, not the sharpest knife in the box, it's hard to get good staff, handed out our flyer (*Special Saturday Offer*).

Bingo. Within minutes, a knock on the window of the van.

'Young man, will you bring my new table to Ranelagh, please?'

'Of course, madam, glad for the bit of work.'

A bit of cringing and forelock-tugging is always an earner. Posh ladies like it.

Table into the back of the van in jig time. Clean white sheet over it. Upmarket, as were our clients. The clean-white-sheet scam became our trademark, after I had robbed every sheet in my mother's house. I got caught and had to buy dozens of them in Guiney's in Talbot Street. Overheads can kill a young business, you know.

Into the gaff.

'I'm a collector,' she said, la di da.

'Our house is Regency,' she said. 'Derek is a barrister,' she said, 'he likes nice things.' Poor Derek.

'Put it over there,' she said. 'What do you think?'

'It would be better under the window,' I said, 'and lose the ornaments. Declutter.'

We moved it.

'You're right,' she said. 'You're a clever young man. What did you say your name was?'

'Cedric,' I lied. There's a taxman behind every sofa. I trade in cash only; tax was what you put on your car. Maybe.

'Cedric what?' she said.

'Cedric McGinty,' I said. I liked the sound of that, I might use it again.

She paid me £5 and gave me a £1 tip.

'What do you think of our collection?' she asked.

'Love it: taste, sophistication, in keeping with your beautiful home,' I said.

She glowed. Guff central. Lying bastard.

'What a lovely thing to say, Cedric, you really are a clever boy, you will go far. I'll book you again see you next week. Can I have a card for a friend?' she asked.

I gave her one with a flourish. She gave me another tip, another pound. Note to self: bigger cards.

And so it began, business boomed, I was run off my feet. Middle-aged posh women everywhere. I had a queue.

'I booked you first, Cedric. My sister is waiting to show you her pieces, we'll book you for the rest of the day.'

Remember, I was a spoofer, a blagger's guide, thirty years before blagging was invented. But I learned fast.

An old dealer saw I was bringing buyers into his shop and in one hour gave me a crash course in Georgian furniture. 'When in doubt, say "Everything after the Regent lost its purity."' It means nothing but stops questions. Perfect. I used it for years.

In one month, one short month, I was rich. Loaded. I had a wedge, wonga, folding, spondulicks, Nelson Eddies, bees and honey, Johnny Cash.

I drank only cocktails with little red umbrellas, Indian takeaways for twenty people, free poppadoms for all. Boots for the footless childer, fur coats for the homeless. Spend, spend, spend.

Then I met the two famous old gay dealers from London, and my real education began. They greeted me on the street. They had diamond earnings, flares, bouffant hair. They came to Dublin to buy good Irish furniture. Antique-trade royalty. They nicknamed me 'Irish'.

They booked me for the day. They were going to a big house auction down the country. I said I would follow their taxi. They said no, they would come with me in the van. I sang for them most of the way and they recited dirty poems. We stopped twice for drinks. I watched them at work that day. A masterclass, no blagging here. Deep knowledge, sophisticated taste, authority, work the room, formidable skill. I soaked it up, steeped my feet.

As they got to know me they told me if I saw anything I liked I was to phone them and describe it to them in detail. They sent a cheque when I bought for them.

All the time I was learning, listening, asking, turning things upside down: why is that? when was that? who made that?

On one of their visits there was a big reception in the city. As always, I brought them everywhere in the van; they just liked it. They phoned me later to collect them. They were a bit drunk. They said a rich heiress had invited a large group back to her house for drinks. A big mansion, gardens lit up, servants at the door, a line of limos. This was fur coat and knickers territory.

I dropped them at the gate. They said, come in. I said, no, it was not my place, they were not my people, I was too young. They said, wait. They came back out, and said the lady had invited me in.

The huge house was dazzling, blazing with lights. Great wealth has its own light, its own seductive pull. Smiling servants.

'Champagne, sir?' asked a young girl of my own age, and then asked with her eyes, What are you doing here?

'I'm with them,' I said, pointing to the two gays. They were wearing matching lilac satin suits.

'Oh,' she said.

'No, no, no,' I said. 'I *work* for them.'

'Whatever,' she said. She left with her bubbles and false smile. You can't win them all.

A senior government minister asked over the noise and music if he could see the famous collection of miniature elephants. Big shots and VIPs everywhere, all asked the same. They all wanted to see them. The lady wavered, but said yes. She also was a little drunk.

She opened the base of a tall bookcase and took out a large square tray with a dark-blue velvet cushion with indents. It held about thirty tiny, jewel-like objects, which burned when the light caught them. This was a world-famous collection. Like all great beauty, it caused a silence to fall and gathered to itself all light.

The lady set out to tell us what each thing was. The best was last. A thirteenth-century Indian elephant, solid gold, four inches long, tiny filigree red pattern across its back. The *howdah* (saddle, to you and me) in diamonds, glittering diamonds, hundreds of them. A little *mahout* (driver) seated with lapis-lazuli-blue turban. Each elephant foot encrusted with precious stones. Those are pearls that were his eyes. The tusks were of ivory tipped with silver. It stood on a bejewelled crystal cushion with pearl tassels all around. People gasped when she held it up to the light. It was dedicated to the loved one of an Indian king. It spoke of a time when there was no limit to labour or measure of cost.

The tray was passed along the extended polished table. Pools of silence followed it. Drinks were served. Finger food. The hubbub started up again. Dancing, people crowding around the trays of food. A ragged sing-song started. Some minutes later the tray came back down along the table on the other side. When it got under the light one thing was missing. The main one. The lady of the house said it was too valuable and fragile for a joke.

'Put it back, please.' Nobody moved, nobody spoke. She said it again, then again, then again.

'Stop the music,' she said, 'turn on all the lights. Put the piece back, now.'

Servants froze, smiles gone. Deadly silence, no one moved.

'Put it back *now*, this is not funny,' she said. A drunk started singing on the sofa. She snarled at him to shut up. Silence again.

After half an hour all were asked to turn out their pockets. Senior barristers, politicians, leaders, no one refused. All done in stony silence.

'I will call the police if this does stop now,' the lady said. No sound, no movement. The police came, took a look at the VIP guests. 'This is a civil matter. We're not getting involved.' They left.

A couple of women were weeping on the sofa. The minister said he had to go as his driver was off shift. Quietly, he left. Two other couples also left. I was told to go and get the van, which I did. The dealers came out and we drove home in silence.

The elephant was never found.

I worked a few years for the two gays. They retired and sold the huge stock of their big Chelsea house, shop and stores. They sold every single thing they had ever owned, every single beautiful thing. Forty years of the best the world had to offer. It made millions. They kept nothing except a little Elizabethan child's silver rattle. It dated from the year when the plague was raging in London. Shakespeare closed his theatre and went touring in that same year.

They bought a big, simple stone Renaissance house in the square of a rough Italian fishing village. They stripped out everything, down to the plaster walls. It was bare and empty, no possessions. Painted in white, filled with light. In the local shop they bought a modest sofa, a table and four chairs and a couple of beds. They would never own anything again. They asked me and my wife to stay with them.

They often rang me. They had breakfast each morning in the square with the locals. They went to the market and bought fish every day as the boats unloaded. They never left the village; it was their home. They bought a tiny second-hand Bambino, which they used to collect their wine from the famous local vineyard, which they owned.

Years passed. I heard from them less, they were old now. One summer morning I got a small box in the post with a beautifully written note. It contained the Elizabethan child's rattle, which had survived, in its innocence and beauty, five hundred years of man's madness. The last thing they owned. They told me I was the son they would have wanted, had they been straight.

They died within weeks of each other. I went with my family to both funerals. They were buried in the small local churchyard. I asked that the rattle be buried with them. They gave the house to the village as a social centre. There was a small photo on the wall, I'm in it with them in the van. That day we were singing the Beatles.

12
T U G

The last two heavy steam tugs in Dublin were built the old way in an English shipyard. Traditional craftsmen's hands working in steel plate and hot rivets. They were indestructible. Curved and flowed with the line of a woman. Shapely. They sat in the water, confident in their strength and beauty. Rakish maybe, gallant certainly.

They were maintained with precision and love and pride and respect for their high Victorian values of lost Empire and Nelson's navy.

The curved and sloping wardroom, saloon and captain's quarters were dressed in polished inlaid mahogany panelling, which glowed in the half light of small green lamps set into the bulkheads. The main table was buffed to a deep shine each day, and all brasswork was turned to gold. Seating was old but well-loved green leather. The floor was oak planking, swept each day so that it shone with wax. The little world of a gentleman's yacht.

There was a main bridge and all-weather topside bridge. Each had a six-foot timber wheel centre stage with brass-capped spokes.

The helm, compass, binnacle, telegraph, all freshly painted and polished, stood to attention, awaiting orders. Along the back wall a bank of pigeonholes, each with brightly coloured signal flags folded to origami perfection with toggles squared away. Behind that the captain's cabin with a daybed. Hospital-nurse-perfect pillows with crisp white sheets and green wool blankets embroidered with ship's name in red. A small brass-bound desk with admiralty charts, binoculars, leather-bound ship's log, all softly lit. A heavy, soft green carpet gave the cabin an unexpected air of comfort. It was a place where men spoke quietly.

The ship's bell seldom spoke but was Brassoed each day and its rope with a monkey knot was blancoed. Question: how many ropes on a ship? Answer: one. The bell rope – all the rest are lines. Remember that, you may be asked.

The stokers worked stripped to the waist. The floor was steel chequered plate, which glowed to burnished pewter from many years of work. All overhead pipework was lagged and painted a blinding white. The sky above a blue hanky in a small grating up on deck. The stoker kicked a hatch and a half ton of coal dropped to the floor at the mouth of the furnace gate. A number nine shovel threw coal to the back of the firebox. Then the door was banged shut and the floor swept. On a stormy night shift, the soft warmth drew an audience of advisers to its wooden bench, wanted or not.

The galley held a long-polished stove. Black as your boots. Big coal fire under deep-grated ovens burnt day and night. Heavy-weather brass piping held rows of scrubbed pots and pans. Knives, racked and razored, marched along the wall. Plates stacked in open baskets. Everything gleamed. All to hand. Ready for action. Stripped down.

No plastic, no convenience-ware in that time. Each day a hot meal was served, bang on time. Table properly laid. Each man with a square, setting out knife, fork, spoon. Centre table a long loaf baked fresh each day, sliced and buttered. Once a week a currant cake. There was jam on Friday. All sat down together, hands washed, no smoking, no reading at table. All proper. After the meal, quiet time, seamen used to long voyages before the time of TV. Men at ease in their own company. Reading, darning, making and mending, hobbies, writing letters, silence for two hours. Dozing. Resting.

The main steam engine. Oh, that most beautiful engine. Gleaming in full traditional colours; green, red, grey. All pipework golden copper and brass. All lagging to white. When working, a noise like a sigh of pleasure. It was hypnotic to watch. You could not look away. You could not look away.

The main beams rocked and nodded. Up and down, up and down. Controlled, ordered, majestic, mighty, splendid power. Called to mind God. It was so quiet you could hear a man talking over it. Finger-clicking rhythm; a woman would sway. Men trailed their hands along it. It was a warm and pleasing to touch. It spoke to you. It was alive. It was loved.

Job on. Big Japanese freighter up coast loaded down to the Plimsoll line. Yokohama, Liverpool, Dublin. Bridge telegraph rang out to engine room. Orders from bridge. All calm, practised, steady. 'Let go for'ard, let go aft, half ahead.' Mooring line coiled. Move away from wall, out into main river.

The westerly wind carried the smoke from the stack downriver, east and ahead of both tugs, out into the blue bay. Our wake, a spill of diamonds across the river gate to the city.

They steamed slowly in convoy. The light that morning would break your heart.

Captain and mate on fly bridge. Full naval uniform, fresh white lids on caps. The captain went to sea at fourteen years of age. Worked on the last four-masted sailing cargo ships up from Australia with wool, when the China tea trade collapsed. He told me that under full sail, a 'cloud of sail' he called it, they could beat any modern freighter across the Indian Ocean. Living history. Went aloft in all weather. North Atlantic winter convoys in the war. Canada to Murmansk in the Arctic circle. U-boats all the way. Slept standing up for two years, torpedoes in the night. Sub-zero. Force Ten. Men who knew no comfort.

Out past lighthouses, port and starboard, old friends. To remember port wine is red. Ship coming up away down on horizon. Both tugs gently turning into a big, lazy three-mile circle to come up under her bow and stern.

Ship's speed to dead slow. Lead tug inches under overhanging bow. High overhead, brown faces appear. Lascar seamen. No words, signs only. The language of the sea. Four-inch manila hawser snakes down from bowsprit and is captured by crew on tug deck. Secured to towing bollard. Looking aft, the captain makes international sign: both arms raised above his head, crossed at the wrists with both fists clenched. 'Made fast, secure, made fast.'

Ship is under tow. New rules now. Tug moves ahead slightly, line takes strain, a dangerous time. Tug settles down into water as weight comes down the line. The heavy wash scourges a deep-purple bruise on the face of the sea.

'All ahead slow' rings out on the bridge telegraph across the sweet, gentle morning air.

The throaty growl of a deep steam whistle booms out across the bay. One blast. 'Stand clear all shipping' and then the silence of a weekday church. Small waves slap the towering knife of the ship's bow high above us.

Flags snap and shiver in the wind, ruffled. The little procession enters port and turns into the berth. Past the old hailing station that long ago had a speaking megaphone, which asked 'What ship are you?' A heaving line shoots out from the deck to the quay. The cowboy lasso uncoils and as it flies is caught by a hogger. Two men release the bitter end and secure to mooring bollard. Ship's winches call in the slack and the ship inches to the quay and softly kisses the shore. Home and dry, safe and sound. Long, mournful blast on whistle, signalling all clear. Tugs let go and turn to home berth. They always lie together. Side by side, a team. Brothers in arms.

Smell of lunch cooking sharpens the air. Stew today, a favourite. Coffee to the captain's quarters. All hands stow and tidy in the silence.

II

13

BITCH DIESEL

'In the name of our Lord Jesus Christ Almighty and his holy and blessed mother this day, get out of that bed or I'll wool you.'

'Don't make me send your poor unfortunate father up those stairs.' My mother shouting from the kitchen. Opening salvo in a daily battle of wits at the start of the day. She's good, I'm better. Sometimes I let her win.

Growing boys need sleep, lots of sleep, warm, cuddly, dreamy sleep. Deep, deep sleepy time. We grow in the night you know. Dreaming gives you a bigger brain, everybody knows that.

'Take it easy, I'm up.' I glide on silent white wings, down and down, back into the glimmering valley of sleep. 'Sleep that knits the ravelled sleeve of care' said the bard. Oh, most wise of men.

What's this. Sudden bitter cold. Oh no, all my warm blankets on floor. The enemy at the gate. A sneak attack, no knock. Messerschmidt at three o'clock, bandits out of the sun. A shocking breach of etiquette in domestic warfare. Falling standards in this modern world.

Breakfast thrown at me. Boiled egg hard. 'This is not my special spoon, where's my egg cup with my initials on it.' I won it for the three-legged race. Soldiers cold. Nothing worse. Dog's abuse.

Then, to put the tin hat on it, this. 'Get out of this house this instant minute and go and help your father who puts the bread on this table.' The final insult, a sweeping brush, yes, the sweeping brush, me and the blameless dog, Knasher, swept out the back door.

My dignity tattered. 'I'm leaving home, I'm going to my auntie's, she knows how to treat a man.' I shouted at the window. My mother danced, a deaf mocking dance, her back turned, radio on loud.

War. Two can play that game.

Instead of work I headed down the road to my best china plate (mate), Nudger. A seer, a futurist, a philosopher, a poet, a good egg, handy with the ladies. First boy on our road with winklepickers. My mother burned mine, an open wound never healed. I mourn to this day. Power and Moore, Talbot Street, the Ted shop.

By the way, I'll tell you what woolling is when my nerves settle and the streets are aired.

We few, we happy few, we band of brothers, Nudger, me, and his cousin from down the country. My people. Nudge lived in a corner house with a big double garage. His father, a senior fitter on the docks, an Olympic gold-metal pilferer. Anything not nailed down, not welded, not hammered home, stuck to him like dog doodoo to an army blanket.

His 'stores' carried every tool, spanner, wrench, pliers, gauge, bolt, screw, washer, nut, known to mankind. Courtesy of a thousand workshops. Little and often, his watchword.

In one corner separated by a wall of pallets, we had started a whiskey distillery as our summer project. Chasing girls, you'd need a money machine. My allowance a joke, an insult to a man of my calibre and standing. All copper piping, heat coils etc, courtesy of Nudge Senior Inc. I was gang leader, Nudge the brains, a natural gifted scientist. A team made in heaven. Talent will out.

Early trials were promising. It drank well, as we say in the trade, with cherry juice and fizzy water. Minor side effects perhaps needed work. Temporary sight loss, but only for some hours. There was an issue with speech. Of course, there are plus and minuses to sight and speech. It's about balance, best not to nit-pick while developing a product.

As the technical work ground on I came up to speed on marketing. I had two working titles 'Gay Abandon' and 'Bitch Diesel'. I know, I know, I know, it was long ago.

We wanted a bottle which stood to attention on a shelf with our competitors. A bottle with presence, a bottle that said, me, me, me, pick me. A bottle show-off. We noted that exotic perfumes sold in such bottles, shapely, elegant, classy, eye candy, in a word, sexy.

What to do.

The apple does not fall far from the tree. The Nudge was a cool, fearless, daring shop lifter. Accomplished, silent, deadly. The cousin Bamber, yes, a smart-arse know-all, dithered over lipstick shades for his mother. Nudge chose a selection of bottles from the back shelves of the ladies' section of the chemist. Cleared shops for miles around. He's now a High Court judge, revered, patrician, sainted. He was on the telly, speaking gravely of crime among the youth.

Our choice fell to a chilled frosted bottle, ribbed, expensive, heavy, perfect.

Not a lot of people know this, but it is difficult to get the smell of perfume out of an empty perfume bottle. Hours of washing in warm soapy water, still Nudge's cat ran for the hills when put to his nose for testing.

Bamber felt our client base were not your regular whiskey drinkers. They might enjoy the 'sight veil' (nice one) also they might like the 'perfume musk' (nice one again) as it brought a whisper of sex to the 'mouth occasion' (yet another nice one). 'We should view the hallucinations and visions as a plus for our youth market,' he said. This was turning into a masterclass in marketing psychology. I forgot to mention the visions etc. earlier, sorry.

The bottle's original contents were called 'Frantic'. French perhaps. Maybe another angle. International sales. Explore. Note to self.

Bamber was sent to seek the views of Big Doreen in No. 27. A girl wise beyond her tender years. Avant-garde radical thinker. She drank a full bottle. Loved it, loved it, loved it all. The sight loss/veil, visions, perfume smell, sex whisper, even the bottle. 'I touched the face of God,' she said. 'Too much is not enough.' Could she invest in our scheme, could she buy a case now for her party?

Success tiptoed on the misty mountain tops. Our little still dripped its liquid gold day and night. Team Nudge/Bamber acquired a stock of 'Frantic' bottles.

Still no killer sales pitch. I put forward 'Get it inta ya Cynthia.' It was voted down as too common.

The launch, an extravaganza. The local park, a bend in the river, wooden park benches, willows trailing in the water. A soft summer evening, the dying of the light guttered and burned low on the river. A sprinkle of stardust, yours truly, a short knock-'em-dead speech.

We set up shop. Our stock, lined up on a table, dazzled and flashed in the evening glow. Launch special offer 2 shillings per bottle. A tasteful hand-drawn sign, *Bitch Diesel what kind of fuel am I?* ran our strap line. Clever, eh!

Nudger's Da had made us a gas ring to cook on. A pan of sausages (cocktail, natch) sizzled and giggled and cosied up to each other. Two pence for three. Value, always value, builds a client base. A transistor played skiffle, girls danced around their handbags. It was a scene man, a scene.

We had sent out invites for twenty-five carefully chosen guests all friends. Three hundred and fifty turned up.

Mayhem. We were victims of our own success. Teddy boys took the sausages, the pan, the gas ring, the lot. They set up at the riverbank. Private party, no sharing. Some people.

Our table knocked over. All bottles stolen by maddened crowd. Profits gone. The drinking started. 'The cherry is crap,' shouted commentary from thieves. Some cheek. I tried to explain this was a private marketing event, I was thrown into the shallow river.

The alcohol kicked in. Frenzied dancing, frenzied fighting. Empties thrown into the river. All our work bobbing gently downstream. My speech notes? Thrown to the wind.

Phase two. Hallucinations, visions, the veil fell. Some collapsed, some cried, some walked into the shallow water calling for their mother. Not so tough now.

Our launch-event site a battlefield. Bodies in all directions. Blind, stumbling drunks, girls crying. Radio played on, the hits. Big Doreen had a new friend up against a tree. The Heimlich manoeuvre. His clothes scattered. Frantic had lived up to its name.

In the distance the *nenaw nenaw* of the half yards in their flashing blue-light Cortina. A quick management review and we legged it home through the back gardens we knew so well. P.S. always plan an escape route.

Back at base, the crushing silence of defeat, of loss, of failure. The air was wounded, hurt. We were dismantling our distillery. 'Fail again, fail better,' said Bamber. Spare me. I wish bleeding Beckett would keep his opinions to himself.

Our dream died on those cold park benches. The willow trees looked the other way. A loser is alone in this valley of tears.

Nudge's mother came home from the shops and into the garage/distillery. 'I was too busy taking out the messages to take my hat off,' she said. 'Turn that truck mirror around to me.'

Why women need a mirror to take their hat off is one of the great mysteries. My father found this endlessly amusing. She pouted her lips and gave herself a little smile. But he liked the ways of women. Oh yes.

She looked at us. 'Why the long face,' as the barman said to the horse. I know it's old but writing eats material. We told her our sad tale. It all tumbled out, there may have been a tear.

'My brave warriors,' she said, 'heads low in defeat.' Oh no, this will never do; this is not the Nudger way. What would Napoleon say, he would say regroup, he would say fight on, no surrender, attack, and so will we.

'I will do one of my high teas.' These were an important event in our social calendar. 'Hop to it, you know the drill,' she said, 'Every man to his task.'

We knew the drill. Wash windows till they sparkled, soapy water to woodwork, light fire and bank up with nutty slack. Hoover kitchen and good room spotless. Polish old leather sofas and pouf. Move square dining table to under window. All hands and faces washed, hair combed, Mrs N lipstick, good red frock. Nice.

By chance the table was exactly the same height and length as the glass. It gave the magical effect that you were floating and eating outside in the garden. A no-nonsense little garden. Two apple trees at the back wall, they gave sweet apples that told of summer sun. Four drills of potatoes covered with horse manure as is proper and right. Then, a worn concrete patch with an old table and chairs. Hose nicely coiled on an old car wheel on the wall. You'd like it.

Inside, Mrs N laid two heavy blankets on the table, then showtime. A large dazzling white linen tablecloth expertly folded and ironed in six-inch squares. It spoke of early Dutch paintings, Vermeer perhaps, Amsterdam school. The unexpected softness to touch and the snowy light thrown up cast a spell never to be forgotten. Table laid with military precision, old knives, forks, mixed but good. Sharp.

She had worked with surgeons in London as a senior theatre nurse. She had picked up some of their posh English ways. Her tipple, as she called it, a gin and tonic. Again, fussy strict protocol. Glass must be polished, fresh ice, only the Dekuypers gin. Their slogan on every bottle, check it. He who Dekuypers nightly takes, soundly sleeps and fit awakes.

She served, perfectly cooked, one egg, one rasher, one sausage, fried potatoes to die for. Homemade white bread, buttered, racked, Toblerone. A large tin teapot with black handle, much used, old and good. You would know it if you saw it. It was from the war. Cups upside down on their saucers. No brown sauce, no ketchup. All proper, all correct, napkins. Polite talk, 'How's your mother keeping?'

Afters, pudding as she called it, English again, a small slice of perfect apple tart with a neat dab of whipped cream. Small silver spoons, much cherished.

Then she sat at the fire and read her favourite, the personal columns, out loud. She had one cigarette, Sweet Afton. 'Quiet lady, own home, good health, widowed, seeks male companionship. Hobbies, embroidery, potholing.' And this. 'Retired settled ex-soldier, pension, seeks lady companion for cycling holidays. Amateur drama, athletics.'

'I often think of their lives,' she said. 'I wonder who I would get, I'd love to meet one of them.' Mr N, made his own arrangements, overtime perhaps.

Then this. Paper down. 'Get out from under my feet, no moping.' She said to me, 'You're the leader, lead. Get a new project, what did you learn at school? Tomorrow to fresh fields and pastures new.' That Mr Milton knew his onions. I put my thinking cap on, as leaders do.

14

POSH TOTTIE

So now. It was the sixties, I was young. All things bright and shiny. First into the sweetshop. My weekend antiques-removal business booming.

'Sorry madam, I am working for Lord Dunberry.' Clients liked that. They waited.

I learnt fast: the basics of furniture, pictures, any good thing. All you need to know is what's quality. Nothing else matters. Keep shtumm in a client's house.

My pub/office/canteen was The Bailey. Poets, fake and real. West Brits, fake and real. Mostly skint. Spoofers, chancers, conmen, failed barristers, actors, mostly resting, landed gentry, mostly skint. Wall-to-wall Trinity students, even professors. My kind of people.

At closing time Duke Street was buzzing. Parties, late-night clubs, hugging, air-kissing. 'Any free houses, darling?'

My uncle's Morris Minor van packed. Fifteen was the record. Once got twelve into an old open MG. Drove around all night, sometimes to three or four parties. Then the early pubs in Capel Street. Drunken singing has its own charm. This was before the seismic discovery that drink affected driving. I was brought up in the old school, where a few pints made you a better driver, more assertive, more assured.

One night Lord Montague, known as His Nibs, called me over to a corner. 'I hear you are sound, young man,' he said. 'Domestics,' he said, 'trouble at mill,' he said, 'meet me tomorrow – somewhere quiet, in the afternoon,' he said.

I met His Nibs. It took three whiskeys to get it out. 'I've fallen madly, wildly, deeply, insanely in love with the Spanish contessa.' Funny how it's never, I've fallen in love with the girl who works in the chipper, the one with the dodgy leg, or the one who takes the money in the carwash.

He'd told his wife that week that they were separating. His wife known to one and all as Nellie. A famous beauty – she was much older than me, I was lovesick – and adored from afar.

She took it well. It was civilized, decorous, refined, even courtly. When he finished and turned around she broke a chair over his head. Nothing serious, four stitches, Aspro, a little lie-down, mild concussion. He got off lightly.

She was going to live in yet another house he owned. They would share the contents of the new house he had inherited on a couple of thousand aching rollers (his little joke). He would move into one wing, with his reduced 'bits', as good furniture is called.

Simple plan. He would engage one of the big removal firms. I would represent Nellie. Each item of silver, paintings, furniture, would be listed and stickered with *his* and *hers* stickers. His choices would be moved into his wing and hers into my vans.

Easy? Yes and no.

When I got to the house on the day, the big remover was there with a fleet. He did not call them vans, they were *pantechnicons*. 'Makes them more important, you can charge more.' He invited me into the back of his biggest pantechnicon, up over the cab. It's called a Luton. A mini hidden office with a kettle, tiny desk, typewriter. He asked to see my quote. He said, 'Foolish boy.' He showed me his. His work descriptions were three pages of guff, mine was one line. 'You need some of my words on your paper. I'll do it now,' he said, and he did. A cute hoor, live in your ear, let the other one out in flats.

His Nibs appeared on his steps. A discreet bandage still on the back of his head. A long string of gummed stickers trailing behind him. 'Nearly ready to start loading,' he said. 'Blue is me, red is her ladyship.'

We started work. I was carrying out a good eighteenth-century library chair, blue sticker. His Nibs was inside. Nellie took the sticker off and shoved it down her bra. 'Put that in your van and cover it,' she hissed. 'If Fuckface thinks that the dago slag is putting her fat arse in my great-grandmother's chair, he has another thing coming.'

I did as I was told, I was following orders. A defence that has echoed down the centuries.

By the end of the day her bra was full (both sides) and so were my two vans. She tore up my loading list so we had no idea what we had. Her Ladyship did. I was ordered to bring my vans and my men to the local pub. Drinks on her. When she arrived in the pub she got a small cheer. Toasted sambos, a rake of pints.

The other lot arrived and set up shop at the far end of the pub. Two camps supporting their champions. Fuckface (it suited him) was not a happy camper. No sign of the Spanish one. Just as well – in the Battle of the Bits, our side had won hands down.

It was getting dark. My orders were to park up in our yard for the night, meet herself at the new gaff in the morning. Nellie was overcome with emotion and gave each of my crew a kiss and a tenner, leaving behind her a trail of broken hearts. Take note, ladies: strategy-wise, kisses and tenners work.

Next morning we arrived at a perfect small Georgian house on the edge of a midlands town. The gates were locked and barred. A note said *Meet me at the front door, alone.* My men went up the town looking for breakfast. I climbed over the wall. On the front door another note. *Meet me round the back.*

She was asleep in the morning sun on the full-size tiger skin we'd 'loaded'. Complete with head, fangs, eyes, tail, blue sticker *Lot 427*, empty champagne bottle. Her kimono fully opened to show her ample charms to the sun. Her breasts was covered with small blue sticker squares. She'd been caught blue-breasted, not red-handed.

I was young, shy, blushing. I said, 'Ahem.' No reply. Then louder, then much louder. She woke up.

'Darling Ced, I knew you would come. Sit down here, beside me. Fuckface and the dago slag have pulled a fast one. I can't get into the house. What will I do, Ced?'

My manly chivalry kicked in. I heard myself say, gallantly, 'Fear not, I will put your bits into one of our warehouses on the QT and drop you off at one of your friend's gaffs.' Men are thick.

'Thank God I have you with me, Ced.' I swelled with pride. I wrapped my coat around her. I hid her bits at the back of a warehouse behind a 2000-ton cargo of pallets. It's not easy being me.

Two weeks later, in our office. 'Lady M is down in the garage looking for you.'

And so she was, surrounded by a ring of admirers and with a big cake that said, 'Thank you, darling boy.' I had interrupted a darts match with a large picture of Fuckface covering the board. Top score was not the bull's-eye but his eye.

'Darling boy,' she said. A little moan, a dog whisper of pleasure from my men. 'I need some things from the shed.'

I brought her in through the cargo and then discovered all her clothes were still packed in the furniture. She took out a half a dozen frocks and shoes and asked me what matched what. Her battered old Land Rover had been driven into the garage by her fan club. Oil changed, quick service, wash, tyres checked. Like I said, men are thick, squabbling over her cake.

These visits became a regular fixture, about once a week. Our men looked forward to them. My drivers showed a talent for picking a bag to match shoes. Who knew? She only left with the full approval of the whole canteen. Every week the Fuckface dartboard became a shrine. I became known the length and breadth of the docks as Darling Boy.

One day I saw the Land Rover outside the warehouse. Behind the forty-foot wall of pallets an upturned tea-chest with a coloured shawl over it, two glasses and a bottle of champagne. Frocks, shoes, handbags scattered all around.

'May I introduce you to the Viscountess Ballybeg. She heard of your gallantry and wanted to meet you, darling boy.' I was unclear if a viscountess was up or down from a lord. Either way, I was now moving in rarefied air at the top of society. No muck here.

'Would it be OK if she played one teeny game of Fuckface darts? The fevered swamps of Ireland's big estates speak of little else. You're a hero.'

Then, 'Good news, the dago slag has been trashed by my cunning lawyer. I now have my keys. I will miss you and this wonderful shed terribly. You must come down with all your men to a barn dance. I will bring all local maidens who are mad for men.'

What an offer. Thank Christ none of my men heard. Can you imagine that day?

She did leave, gloom came over the yard. She was deeply missed. Men boasted of their score at Fuckface darts and told of silver they'd hidden. There were fights over who she liked the best.

One day I was going into work. A tanker coming out the gate, Nellie in the cab. She shouted down, 'Micko is going to Sligo and said he would bring me for a spin, I can stay and hunt with Lord Classymore. How trilling?'

Micko wisely gunned the big tanker before I could comment. He told me later he was concerned only with client satisfaction. She went all over Ireland by heavy tanker, hunting, possibly.

In the yard a 'Slygo' became the new word for an outing with a lady. Debate raged over whether he got the rub of the relic. His a stony silence except to confirm that Fuckface darts was indeed famous in the big houses of Ireland.

Here's how it all ended. Lord M met me often. The contessa brought over her mother. I cannot write down what he called her. 'Tricky,' he said, 'tricky.'

He whispered he missed Her Ladyship. I did not mention the darts. Nellie became a leading socialite, her little Georgian manor a magnet for rock stars and celebrities. The dago slag, her mother and extended family moved out of the big house. No stickers this time. No battle in the pub. Me and His Nibs went for a quiet pint.

'Your sheds are famous in our little world,' he said. 'Could I hold my art exhibition there?'

I mumbled about insurance. 'My daubs,' he called them. Never a truer word.

Nellie got married again to a multimillionaire Yank. She heard a driver calling him 'the septic tank' in docklands slang. She called him The Septic from that day. The wedding was the event of the year. Posh tottie, head office. It was a giant barn dance. The cake was a ten-foot-long tanker truck. Guess where it was held.

15

WEDDING TACKLE

Thursday night, the pictures, written in stone, me, the Nudge, the cousin. The club 'sock' money at a low ebb. Our budget, cheap seats, one popcorn, three pints of cider. We'd started to drink. Being under age was a problem, like all problems, a solution can be found.

A cowboy picture. Why do the Indians always lose. They have the best hair. Those little square hankies they wear front and back, what are they for? That inscrutable gazing into the clouds. Don't talk a lot, your Indian. Love the single-feather look at the back of the head.

The best joke I heard from a teacher. Daryll Zanuck (great name) was given the complete works of Shakespeare. Next day he said, 'What a guy, and he wrote all that with a feather.' Now that's funny.

For our cider we went to an old railway hotel near the docks. It had a bar out the back for locals. The Mutton Dagger. The barman asked what age were we. I pointed to each one: eighteen, eighteen, nineteen.

'We lead pampered lives, no hardship, ruined with the kindness, not a mark on us.' 'Whatever.' He was tired of life or I had lost my audience, or both.

'Three pints of cider, please. Have you any free nuts?'

'No.'

'Have you any free stuff?'

'No.'

'Three packets of crisps please, salt and vinegar.'

There was a lot of noise and music coming from the big function room.

'What's on?' I said.

'Big wedding, two hundred punters going mental, full band, free bar, dancing.'

We took the cider to our 'table'. Here's a good tip. Open crisp bag fully down each side and spread out. It's like a little picnic, makes them more important. Crisp packaging needs to be looked at. Maybe, a round bag that turns into a little plate. The blue paper with salt could have jokes or wise sayings. A missed opportunity. I'm an ideas man.

Six men entered like cowboys into a saloon. The wedding had come to us. The second pale sherry was evident. New suits, mohair, Brinylon, no ties, hair oil. Suits straining over bellies, if a button went would take your eye out.

'Six small ones,' the lead reveller said.

'Certainly, sir.'

'Put them on the tab next door.'

'Certainly, sir.'

'And give those three young fellas a drink.'

'Certainly, sir.'

'And nuts,' I said.

'And crisps,' Nudger said.

No *certainly sir*, this time. We got free nuts, two bowls, big.

'Come over here and tell me no lies. Whose father are you?' We joined our new friends, got stuck into the nuts just to annoy laughing boy at the bar. Two pints later. He was a pork butcher, two shops.

'There's money in pigs, I kill my own. Best black pudding in Dublin. Queues every Saturday. I'm thinking of exporting to France. The Frog loves his pudding.' 'Poshpud, what do you think?'

'Inspired,' I said. And it was, and he did, it made millions.

'I have your first slogan,' I said. '*When all of a sudding, we ate Irish pudding.*'

'I like it, needs work, but I like it. I will give you fifty pounds if we use it.' And he did. The Frog did not understand the joke, but loved it. It became his company logo.

We were roaring laughing. A large lady put her head around the door. Frock like the curtains and swags of the Savoy cinema we had just left. The hat, more feathers. The face, Mount Rushmore, the one on the left, the big one.

'Dazzler, the bride is giving out that you're in here.'

Dazzler? His real name was Micky, love it.

'Five minutes, blame these young fellas.' They drank up. 'Come in for a drink lads, there's a load of young ones in there who'd love to throw you around.'

'But we're not invited,' I said.

'You are now.'

In. A blast of showband music. The evening was at the later, more informal stage. Competing sing-songs, women sitting on men's laps, arm-wrestling, children under tables. Jiving, throwing shapes, old ladies ballroom dancing. The band played on, hard men, seen it all. Never stop playing, no matter what happens, never stop playing. Like life.

Another request from Dazzler to the one he loves. He who pays the piper calls the tunes. Mount Rushmore took a shy bow.

Let me telescope the next two hours into what we drank as we table-hopped as honoured guests of the father of the bride. Crème de menthe, Babycham, cocktails (various) sherry, pale and sweet, vodka, gin, whiskey, schnapps. We went along the top rail of the bar. Every bottle sampled. We felt no pain, we strode the earth, we were the match of any man.

Later, much later, I sang my Val Doonican medley, new moves. A crowd-pleaser, I sat on the bride's mother's knee.

One a.m. Now I'm now at the top table. I have been 'given' a tiara, blue and cream flowers intertwined. It suited me. I had swapped my leather jacket with a bridesmaid for a cape, no, not a cape, you know the round thing the

Pope wears, like a big brolly without the spokes. That. White satin, random pearls, a row of small white furry balls around the edge. Think Elvis, Vegas, late period.

A wide-ranging conversation with the bride about sex. It turned out she was English. A spotwelder in an aircraft factory like her mother and granny before. A good, high-skilled job. Respect.

A detailed description of the spotwelding protocols on the wing of a Wellington bomber – gave it its legendary strength – set out expertly with knives and forks as spars and napkins as wing fabric. I wish my father could have heard it. What a woman. I could see a spotwelder as the mother of my children.

To end. A ceremonial fight, as is traditional and right. Battle lines drawn, the pork-butcher camp, the spotwelder camp. Much chest pushing.

'Don't call me a gobshite, you gobshite.'

'You, outside, leave my mother out of this.'

'Remember the famine.'

'I never touched your sister, she jumped me.'

'Yeah, you and whose army.'

The pork butcher called for single combat, again, as is tradition and proper. Two big men stepped forward, champions of their clans. Brinylon open to the waist. Our man swung a looping punch, lost his balance, in effect knocked himself out. I switched sides, who backs a loser? Helped to carry our winner in a victory lap around the hall. I have no further memories from that point of the evening.

Time passed.

Light filtered into my brain. My eyes would not open. My head and hair was welded to a nylon carpet with a thick caked soup plate of hardened vomit. The texture of a cheap rubber toy left too near the fire. I pulled my head free. The ripping, tearing sound of Velcro. I may have lost skin, damaged my looks.

I turned slowly, Nudge and the cousin were in bed, snug, two spoons, fully dressed under a mound of overcoats. Sleeping like babes.

My pain, my pain. I staggered to the toilet, ripped a truck hubcap of vomit from the side of my head, more Velcro. That it should come to this.

Mrs N walked in. 'Follow me,' she said. She filled a hot bath while I sat dazed, watching her.

'Get in, wash yourself well, put these on.' She handed me clean pajamas. She took me into their spare room. A small bed, white covers, white sheets, white pillow. As always with her, perfect. She turned down the blanket, I slid into delicious sleep even as I was talking to her. The coolness of those sheets are with me to this day.

I woke mid-afternoon. Mrs N was standing over me with one of those little trays with legs, for sick people.

A boiled egg, two small slices of toast, a pot of tea, one cup, one saucer. I sat up, she sat on the end of the bed. 'Are you a basher or a cutter?' she said.

'A cutter,' I said, as I cut the top off my egg down low. A little corner of butter, pinch of salt, plunged my teaspoon deep into the egg, made sure I got a little yellow, a little white, a little butter. The spoon made a sucking noise as it came out. Turned it upside down onto my buttered toast, placed carefully into my mouth. The rest is silence.

I drank my tea and we chatted as the light failed. The taunts of the gang 'other mammy' were true that day.

I cried for a week when she died. I often think of her and that perfect golden afternoon she gave both of us. She was my friend, and I hers. As I said before in these little stories, love hurts.

16

B . S . A .

My father was old school. Do things once, do things right. No short cuts. Once a year he took a week to himself to strip and rebuild a big engine from a 44-ton tractor unit. It was like a retreat for him. He worked in silence; the yardman knew not to prattle.

This is what was done. Garage was swept out with care. Any grease and oil on the floor was scrubbed down with warm soapy water. The walls were roughly whitewashed so that light poured down from the heavens. The heavy wooden work benches lining each wall were stripped and covered with fresh newspapers. The watchman's brazier was lit and six sacks of fuel were stacked alongside. One for each day, no more, no less.

The big truck outside had its cab tilted forward so that the engine, gearbox, chassis, were fully exposed. This was power-washed with a steam lance so that all grease and road dirt washed away.

The paintwork shone as new. Spick and span. Then, and only then, the truck was rolled into the bay and over the pit below. Fresh overalls to each man.

A heavy steel toolbox was wheeled in, padlock opened. Woe betide any man who touched another man's gear.

As each tool came out it was rinsed in warm soapy water, dried, laid out in size sequence, cascading down in order, proper order. Spanners, sockets, ratchets, wrenches, hammers, pliers, punches, all precise, all to hand. All present and correct. Tried and tested. Tickety boo. It was a pleasure to watch.

The stripping of the engine began. As each piece was removed it was handed to the yardman who took it out to a big old stone basin of fresh petrol. It was dropped in to steep for a few minutes, then gently cleaned with an old soft brush. Each time a little miracle. Every trace of grease and dirt gone, new, shining, bright steel gleaming in the light of day. It was then laid out along the benches on the newspapers to dry, in the order it came out. In two days the benches wore a glittering crown of factory-new pistons, engine blocks, camshafts, injectors, pumps, shafts. The gearbox lay open, its most intimate secret parts exposed, complex, mysterious, unknowable.

Then the man from the machine shop arrived in his brown shop coat and cap. Every piece carefully calibrated, some passed, some failed. All that failed thrown into the scrap for Davy Frame Hammond Lane. All else machined and polished by hand, ready for reassembly.

He and my father sat on old truck seats with a cable-roll table in the back of the garage beside the warm fire. Comfortable as the day, snug. They chatted over mugs of tea and ham sandwiches from an old biscuit tin, held with clean brown paper. A good fitter never has dirty hands or overalls. When he put a spanner to a nut it seemed to open to please him, there was no effort. When he picked up a piece to refit, 'offering up' it was called, it always 'fell' to its rightful place. Precise, easy, slow, old knowledge passed down father to son, man to man. Proper.

The big engine block was lifted out by an overhead block and tackle and swung gently in the air. The hanged man. It could be moved around by a finger as work was done. When the rebuild was finished he got somebody else to start it up. A little bit of showing off. That's allowed.

At the other end of the yard by the river our first summer gang meet in the old Chevy. Full house. An amazing piece of business, top of the agenda. Snag's brother had got a motorbike, a motorbike. B.S.A. British Small Arms, used to make guns. Lovely.

An ancient B.S.A., messenger boy's bike, rickety, rackety, rusty, but a motorbike, an actual motorbike. Everybody of course, would get a 'go'.

When my turn came I sat into the saddle, the big old engine thudding below me. I gently eased the rubber grip back and to my delight glided forward with the greatest of ease. I leaned left and floated soft and slow in a dream state around the big concrete yard. I have not known the joy of being alive more than in that moment of a boy's soaring ecstasy.

I wanted one. I wanted one. We siphoned petrol from vans into lemonade bottles and spent a glorious sunlit morning riding around in circles singing woman-trouble songs. Heaven, heaven, heaven.

Where did the bike come from? Could we get one? Talk of tours of Ireland; we could build a wall of death, make a fortune. Gang sat piled up on top of each other in the big back leather seat of the Chevy. In the pin-drop silence, this we heard.

An auction was held in the yard of an old Georgian house out past the airport. Government surplus, diggers, compressors, vans, trucks, scaffolding, dumpers. It sold ex-P and T equipment, that's where the bike came from.

An immediate gang decision, we would go to this place. All piled onto the back of an empty trailer heading north. We banged the roof of the cab at the big house. The driver pulled in, we jumped off at the junction, two-minute walk, we found it.

Farmers, wide boys, Travellers, dealers, small builders, conmen, whispering, conniving, plotting, talking behind their hands. Fool's gold.

In a far corner under an old canvas we found the motherlode. A heap of old B.S.A. bikes, rusted, battered, with a mountain of spares, engines, wheels, marked *job lot*. 'Take as found. No guarantees no refunds.' Treasure. We went to the 'refreshments area', an ancient sagging caravan, flat tyres sunk into the ground. A caravan that came to die. The woman, large, blonde, big blonde, bright lipstick, the arms of a wrestler. Her Burco boiler sent out little wisps of steam.

'How much would it be for four doughnuts and four teas, miss?' She liked it.

'Two shillings,' she said, a little smile, she flexed her muscles.

'Four teas and two doughnuts, miss,' I said. 'We have to keep our bus fare home.'

When she got our order she handed me two big cream slices, the expensive ones. 'Don't tell my gaffer.' She smiled her little smile again. 'My mother would like you, miss,' I simpered. With women, you either have it or you don't.

The sale started. The auctioneer, standard big orange cattle-dealer's boots, heavy cap, comb-over, belted brown coat. Biro tied to his board with a string. He moved around the yard, stood in front of each lot, big voice, banged the hammer on the nearest thing, sometimes a buyer's head. It always got a laugh. Then us.

'Scrap bikes, what am I bid?' he called out across his meagre audience. A small voice at the back said, 'Two pounds.' It was me. 'Sold, to the woman with the wooden leg.' A tired half laugh, he needed new material.

A friend who had bought a small truck said he would bring our new purchases home. We loaded all the spares, and towed two bikes home with a heavy rope. I steered one. I was Caesar riding in his chariot into Rome. No wonder they needed a slave to run beside them to remind them they were mortal.

After a full day's work we got one bike started, perfect, except no brakes. We were riding it on waste ground by the river beside an old dock with a two-foot pipe crossing it. Over this pipe was a narrow work gantry. It crossed about twenty feet of deep water. With no warning, Nudger gunned the engine and raced full speed to the gantry and roared across the open water. Shock, fear, speechless, silence. He rode around the back of the dock, stepped off the bike. We were struck dumb. Hanging in the air, the ancient and oldest question since man saw bravery in battle as the measure of each man. Who next? Who now? I stepped back, Snag stepped forward, got on the bike, gunned the engine, hit the gantry hard, too hard. He was thrown off down into the dark water far below. The bike floated a few seconds in a halo of dazzling sunburst colours from the oil, then sank quietly. Snag, drifting down with the flow, his small shout lost. A work boat came alongside and caught him. With difficulty they pulled him aboard. He was a lucky man to be alive.

A local driver gave us a lift back to the yard. Chastened, frightened, no bluster now.

Next day we met, work on bike stopped. Woodbine break. A yardman started up a big D9 Caterpillar bulldozer. Forty tonnes, big as a wartime tank. It made the noise of war-movie tanks as its steel tracks clanked across the concrete yard. Dozers don't steer, they turn by stopping one track so that it lumbers and lurches around. He headed for the corner. The heavy tracks ground over the bikes, the spares, the wheels, the tyres. Then it pivoted around on one track, the squealing tortured metal torn asunder. He stopped the machine and turned off the engine.

Total silence.

My father said, 'A young man was nearly killed yesterday from stupidity. You have no judgement yet, you are too young to have powerful bikes, you have no insurance, no tax, no licence, no sense. Get this lot cleaned up and out of my yard now or your gang hut will be next. I want it spotless.'

We had met power and authority head on. No ifs, no buts. At the end of a long day's work we retreated to the Chevy. 'If one person says fail again, fail better, he's out of the gang,' I said. Snag said, 'The Buddha tells us all things must end.'

'Jesus,' I said. 'Give me strength.'

17

PAN

Saturday was go-into-town day. Get-out-of-the-house day. Get-away-from-grown-ups day. Bus stop, quick check of gang money, the sowck money. Set the day's agenda, squabble over the top-deck front seat on bus, the television seat.

Clerys clock, up to the big café, top floor. One slice of cake, four forks, wander around the shop. Across the river, Trinity College, Book of Kells. Why don't they put numbers on the pages, so you know what you'd seen before? Down Henry Street, love the crowds, into Moore Street.

'Four for a pound, missus.'

Love the shouting, love the life force, love the city. Down Mary Street into Capel Street, donkey jackets, work boots, overalls shops. More crowds, people being alive, just alive, just living.

Fruit market, full circuit, over to the banana man.

'Don't tell me,' he shouted, 'your mother ran off with a sailor, your little brother has rickets, you're starving, any free stuff?'

He gave us a big bunch of brown bananas, they were lovely. He asked the man in the next stall had he any 'bruised fruit'. Good name for our skiffle group. He gave us a big bag of 'bruised' apples.

'Waste not want not,' the man said, 'I hope your mother is happy, life is short.' A fruit-selling philosopher.

Cross the Liffey at Parliament Street, up to Dublin Castle, saw where they hanged men in castle yard. Up to the Daisy Market in Francis Street. We knew all the dealers.

'Hello Madge,' 'Hello Sadie,' 'Hello Cissy.'

Cheap clothes, bric-a-brac, pots and pans, huge stacks of washing power, why always washing powder? Down at the back, our man. His goods today would be called militaria. Small, weary, furtive, the eye of a concerned rodent, broken English. Soldiers' uniforms, helmets, bits of rifles, empty shells, bullets, army belts, holsters, medals, boots. Boys love war, machine guns, ammo, Germans, submarines, destroyers, torpedoes, ackack. Old war movies,

'Carry on, number one.'

'Steady as she goes.'

'Gerry is busy tonight.'

'Action stations.'

'Take that, Fritz.'

'Share that among you, blockheads.'

He told us his name was Gunter, if you believe that you believe anything. Lean forward, look in all directions, hushed voice.

'New material, secret, I should not have this.'

He showed us German commando daggers, beautifully made, polished steel blade, brass-ribbed handle for grip, Swastika stamped into hilt, dated 1941. Balanced, light, dangerous. We bought two.

'Tell nobody,' he hissed. We swore. We slid them into their sheath, then into our belt. Deadly. But everyone knows I'm a squealer.

Down Engine Alley into Meath Street via the grotto. Over to Victoria Quay to watch the Guinness steam barges loading. Beautiful things, I miss them on the river.

'Bring us for a spin, mister. We'll polish your brassoes.'

Lazy wisping steam, this way and that in a light breeze from the little funnel.

'You're too young,' was shouted back, 'too dangerous, we could be torpedoed at Capel Street Bridge, no survivors, what would we tell your mother?'

I saw inside the little cabin once. Cosy, tight, little coal stove smiling bright. Proper sensible kettle, row of mugs. Out tiny porthole, hoist of wooden barrels landed snug into the hold with a woody bump. Easy as kiss your hand, 240 hogsheads per voyage.

My dream job, captain of the *Killiney*, my favourite barge, delivering Dublin's finest to a wide, waiting, grateful world.

Walking back to town down the river we noticed Merchants Arch for the first time. Straight in, turned right and into a world we never knew. Temple Bar.

Then, it was a derelict forgotten desert in the inner city. Most shops boarded up, cobbled streets and lanes deserted, not a sinner, not a soul. Heaven.

We found an abandoned factory in a Georgian house, the door was damaged and tied with string.

In like Flynn.

Ground floor, broken machinery, drums of oil, rubbish, rude graffiti, sheets of wallpaper hanging like sails in a calm. Wooden stairs. Up. Store rooms, piles of clothes, packing cases piled high. More stairs, up again. Surprise. A big roomy flat looking out over rows of slate roofs following the slope down to the river. How many souls had looked out over that lovely view in three hundred years. The fateful departed.

Three bedrooms, one locked, bottles everywhere, broken furniture, grimy windows. A weary old sofa. All hope gone. Sag central, another one on its back. Big fireplace full of bottles and old papers. Heavy timber floor. Instant home, ideal home, love at first sight.

We pulled the old sofas into a nest of broken seating around the fire. Cleared the grate and lit the fire with broken timber.

A place to call our own. A roof over our heads, you can't beat bricks and mortar.

Excited, planning we would come back tomorrow for a slap-up picnic, a blow-out, a tightener. Must re-member to bring candles, a frying pan. When we left we tied the door up again with the string. On the bus home we agreed who would bring what. Big adventure.

Next morning, buzzing. Sausages, check. Two loaves, check. Butter, check. Jam, check. Ketchup, check. Apple tart in silver paper, check. Lemonade, check. Four bars Aero, check. Two big flasks hot tea. Ice cream for afters to be bought in Dame Street.

To each man a small haversack, said we were going on a hike. Back in the same door, found old crate and set up on tea chests in from of the fire. Lit fire, love fire. Laid out all food properly, no picking allowed. All scrap into fire. We played families. Everybody wanted to be mother. Nudge got it. The senior man. I was the eldest son. We put on 'voices'.

'How was your day, darling?'

'More tea, vicar?'

'Cricket rained off again.'

'New frock, mummy?'

'Perfect, perfect day.'

In the middle of a good laugh, a heavy scraping noise from the locked room. Sudden fear, frozen. Deep instant silence. Heavy feet dragged across a bare timber floor. Shuffling to the door. Menace. Brass knob jiggles, key turns in rusty lock, door swings open.

We had all stood up in fear, two smallest behind me and Nudge.

'The daggers,' I whispered.

As we took then out, a big man stepped into the room. Breathing stopped. Tall man, long, matted, dirty hair, weeks of stubble, sad sad eyes, broken teeth, filthy torn shirt, braces, one up one down, ragged trousers, bare feet, dirty and bloodied.

Stunned long silence, each man staring at the other.

'What are you doing here?' he whispered, hoarse. I held up my dagger.

'This is my granny's house, what are you doing here?'

'I have been sleeping here for weeks.' A long silence. He swayed a little.

'I did not know you were here. I am very hungry, I have been sick for days here on my own. I'm sorry I frightened you, can I have some of your food, or I will faint.'

I picked up a ham sandwich and handed it to him, my dagger still up. It was gone in seconds.

'Can I have another?' Gone!

'Are you thirsty?' I said. I handed him a bottle of lemonade, he put it to his mouth and drained it.

'Sorry,' he said, 'do you want me to go?'

'No,' said Nudge, 'sit down and share our food.'

He did, he was a gentle person, a wounded person.

'Have I frightened you? I am sorry, I have been sick here on my own for weeks, I am truly sorry.'

Midge asked, 'Would you like a hot four-sausage sandwich with a nice mug of tea?'

He began to sob. I put a coat around his shoulders. I asked could I get his boots. I saw he had been sleeping on the floor. He put them on, no socks.

Things settled down, we ate in silence for a while. He ate his sausage sandwich like a starving animal, which he was.

'Sorry to eat so much of your food. Tell us who you are,' Skin said. A silence. He spoke for two hours.

Spellbound. He spoke well, he spoke soft, he spoke low. A life shattered, all the usual suspects, drink, drugs, bad choices, bad luck, just dumb bad luck. A loser.

The old sun to the west struggled through the dirty windows and rotten lace curtains, made yellow shadows across our little gathering.

We lit our candles, and listened to a broken soul reaching out for help. Even as boys we knew it was a message as old as time, as old as mankind, an SOS to the heart. Twice he cried, once he dozed for a moment. We waited in silence, we knew.

His father was a wealthy man. A big hardware business across Cork. He was an only son. He did not want to sell shovels for his life. He wanted to be a priest. A bloody fight with his father, started drinking, left home. Went to a seminary for four years, gave up with one to go. Stole money from his father's business, went on a one-year bender. More stealing, trouble with the police. His father threw him out on the street. He met a girl, drug addict. Soon he was too. Arrested, jailed for twelve months, released six weeks ago. Then today, here, sick, broken. He ate most of the food. He cried softly from time to time. Two of us held his hands. He dozed; we sat in silence and waited. The light failed.

'God sent you to me today, your goodness has saved me, I will never drink again. I will go to my father's house and beg his mercy and forgiveness. I will lead a quiet life in penance for the suffering I have caused my father and mother.'

He gave each of us a gentle, silent hug, a face wet with tears. He would stay here and get a few weeks' casual labouring work to pay for a second-hand suit. He would have a haircut and shave before he went to the house of his father.

We said we would bring in our gang savings, he said no. We left him our bus fares. We would walk home. We gave him our frying pan.

As we parted he said we would meet at this place, this day, at noon in one year. This we did and every year since. To the minute.

He turns up now as Father Mick Darcy. A big strong healthy man. He has since married two of us and said the prayers to bury our fathers and mothers.

He told us his father was filled with joy when he returned home. He blamed himself and his pride for wanting a bigger business. Their lives from that day were blessed with the deep love of a father for his son.

He told us our frying pan saved him. He would never have thought of cooking on the fire. Take a bow, Nudge. He still has it as his most cherished possession.

He sold the big business when his father died and gave the money to the poor, for he was now rich.

When he wanted to pray he fried an egg on the pan and thanked God for the day that he met us. Our frying pan, imagine that.

18
BOOT

My grandfather owned seven pairs of brown boots. All leather, all matching, all bought same day, same shop. Size eleven. He rotated them. Each pair worn for one day, then rested. This meant laces out before they were put away in a line-up out of the sun. His boots were polished every evening as he steeped his feet in hot water with salt from the chemist.

He had fourteen pairs of matching wool socks (white) and fourteen pairs of laces (brown). He washed his socks and laces after he polished his boots.

He was fond of his feet.

Polishing was done in silence. He put his closed fist into each boot to lift it and hold it upside down. He used only a large drum of brown polish he got from a friend in the army. He used a small pointed brush to apply polish. He let the boot 'sit' for ten minutes, then polished hard with a heavy coarse brush.

The job was finished with a 'heel ball', a hard, round, black ball of wax. This was rubbed to the back of the heel to give a sharp shine. The Dublin saying 'heelball' comes from this, i.e. taking extra care of your turn-out. The whole boot was then gently rubbed with a soft chamois for 'finish'.

On certain summer Saturdays he scalded a large gallon white enamel jug and a white mug. He scalded everything he used, knife, fork, spoon.

'Boiling water kills all,' he said.

He walked to the local pub, had the jug filled with Guinness, walked home. He brought out two chairs and the newspaper to the little garden at the front of his red-brick house in a quiet Dublin street. He read his paper in the sun and drank from his scalded mug.

Neighbours who were passing got a drink from a cup and sat down for a chat. Old friends in a quiet street in the sun of a city and a life now gone.

He placed one bet every Saturday. An each-way treble accumulator carefully written out and wrapped around the money for the bookie. The small boy who ran to the betting shop got a bar of chocolate for his trouble. My grandfather paid the wager but if it won he shared with the whole street. All took a keen interest, the radio sang out from many windows to bring joy or sorrow to the street.

He had an unusual job. He acted as local agent for a French firm that made some of the earliest luxury cars. They sold a handful each year. He was their man on the ground. They were shipped in wooden crates. He collected from the docks, prepared them for delivery to the new owners. Petrol, water, air pressures, batteries.

Most buyers then could not drive so he brought the car to big estates and wealthy farms around Dublin. He stayed a few days to teach the owner how to service, maintain, drive. They often called to see him when they were in Dublin. He taught wives and daughters to drive, some became friends.

One incident got him sacked. The top of the engine head was sealed with ornate brass nuts. Brass is soft. To avoid it being marked he insisted that a cloth be put over the nut so that the spanner did not mark it.

One buyer, a rich titled person, refused to do this and marked the brass nut by using the wrong-sized spanner with no cloth.

My grandfather refused to deliver the car to him. The buyer told him to get off the estate and take his car with him.

He was told by his boss to bring the car back and apologize to his Lordship. He refused. Many powerful customers wrote and said they wanted him back.

Word of the incident went all the way up to the owner of the large French firm. He was told that their strange Irish man had refused a car to a lord and told him he was not fit to look after it. The owner of the car firm said my grandfather was quite right. He was reinstated with a rise and a bonus. He stayed with them for many years. The tale sold many cars. A letter of support was written by the president of the French company to all customers.

When he died, his boots, socks, laces, polish, brushes, heelball were put into a clean hessian sack and buried with him. Lords and ladies came to his funeral. He was buried in his bare feet so that they could be admired by all. He was fond of his feet.

19
S I D

My mother shouted.

'The cat is going up the stairs to you, he wants his ears rubbed, he likes the left one first then the right, send him back to me for his Horlicks and cream.'

The cat ruled the house with an iron fist in a purring, cuddly glove.

Sid, our cat, first laid siege to our house with a simple but deadly plan. He sat in the middle of our garden gate in the cold and rain for three days and three nights. I was sent out with the sweeping brush to scare him away. He sat on top of the gate post and peered down with mild interest. As soon as the hall door closed on my retreat, he was back on station.

Next night I was sent out with a bowl of milk. Ignored. We learned that his preference was Horlicks (not Ovaltine) and fresh cream (whipped). Second night, heavy downpour, whole family looking out the window. Vigil. The cat sat in the rain as the veil of darkness fell.

He stared back at us, blank, no expression, no movement. Looking, silent, still. Inside, debate raged; one extreme view, we should get him put down. Tears, near blows.

Third night rain, all resistance crumbled, surrender. The front door was left open; we retreated to the good front room, turned off the light. Neatly, daintily, with slight hesitation, he walked as if on a knife edge, tight-rope to the door. Entered sniffily, mincing. Maybe, maybe not. Down the hall, rubbing along the wall into the big old kitchen. We had a proper warm Aga. He headed to its heat as a guided missile seeks its target. He sank in front of its yellow doors and took leave of his body. Legs splayed to the warm stone floor as if he no longer owned them. Flattened, stretched, all life gone, a sad old carpet. Tattered, no eyes, no ears. A Davy Crockett hat.

'Poor little thing,' my mother said. 'We will let him stay tonight until that heavy rain clears.'

'Hah.'

Doreen from number twelve sent down a wicker basket and blanket. This was scrupulously ignored. An unspoken message, loud and clear. This cat sleeps where he chooses. Any hour of day or night. If that is in the middle of the room then stepping over him is the house rule.

Slowly, slowly, he gained control as a tide swarms up a flat beach. No matter how hard you look you cannot see its advance.

Sidney was his name. No memory of how this came about. Sidney it was and ever shall be. There was a minor problem. Sidney was a lady. Doreen was the local sage on sex, sex problems, marriage good and bad, courtship, love affairs, babies, births, death and all ladies' troubles and issues. She was a cloak and dagger whisperer. A *Guinness Book of Records* tea drinker. 'A colour of milk and half a teaspoon of sugar, thank you, pet.'

Her place by our Aga a listed structure, post no bills. 'That's Doreen's seat, you pup.'

One night, without warning, she threw her coat over an outraged Sid. Cat caught napping. Lifted him upside down caught up in the coat. Pulled his legs apart to look at his wedding testimonials. Every man in the room flinched and crossed his legs.

'Just as I feared,' she said like Sherlock Holmes. 'Your Sid has not meat and two veg. He's a miss.'

Black hatred was the look to the woman who had dared to defile him/her.

What to do. After much agonizing it was formally agreed Sid would remain Sid till the end of time and stay in our house until he/she chose what to do. That choosing took twenty years.

Things settled. Time passed. Sid could work a room. Just when you were the favourite she would slowly, formally rise from your lap with a look that was rueful, disappointed, regretful. Climb onto another lap with a questioning little gaze up at the new love object.

She lived a long comfortable life. Ruthlessly selfish each and every day. But with charm, great charm. Mice were beneath her attention. They roamed free until we set a trap. Her male admirers up and down the road vied for her affections. The top of our back wall was a clothesline of sad suitors sick with love. Every man will know that pain of love rejected with a haughty look of contempt and a turned back.

She spread her charms discreetly, sparingly, ladylike, always ladylike.

'Kittens, kittens, four kittens under the stairs, four kittens, four kittens, four kittens,' little Lilly from next door, trembling with excitement, ran screaming through the house.

And there were. Four bald, blind scraps of life. The gift of life itself, in a corner, on an old coat under the gas meter. Mother lay beside, eyes milky, eyes dreaming. The most sacred mystery of new life, the old and ancient secret of the circle of birth and death. One big wheel turning, passing life on, and on, and on. Death is only life by another name.

I looked into her eyes, what did I see. Deeper than intelligence, deeper than all things we know. Her body held the knowingness of millions of years of evolution. She did not think, no need. Listen to the code, the body will know. Hunt, kill, eat, sleep, reproduce, repeat. Again hunt, kill, eat, sleep, reproduce. Carry on your tribe, your race. Winner takes all. Each generation follow the code. Down and down, the millions of years. Survive, survive, survive, that's the job in hand.

She died as she had lived, on her own terms. Take it or leave it. We live beside a canal. She walked its path every day of her life. One day, full of age and pain, her job done, she walked into the water and was gone.

The lock-keeper found her, she was unmarked, asleep, curled and cosy. Ladylike, always ladylike. A hand grenade of grief hit our house. Sid, Sid, Sid, why did you do that, but we knew, of course we knew.

George, the lock-keeper, said cats go when they want to go. No sadness, look to the kittens; they survive. Life survives; again, death is only life by another name.

She was buried under a sunny, south-facing old brick wall. A freshly ironed cotton pillow slip, a tin of Horlicks. Neighbours came, a little party. 'Remember when she this, remember when she that.'

We put up a proper little grave stone and it said only this: *Sid forever.*

20
H I H O

It's true the darkest hour is just before dawn. Driving home, 5 am, tired to the bone. Longing for 'sleep that knits the ravelled sleeve of care'.

An empty east-coast side road down to the shoreline, to my left a small rocky cove with a finger of sand. First light of dawn peeping up over a faraway horizon. A sea of shadows and troubled whispers. The scimitar blade of the earth's curve plain for every man to see. Splintered golden light flared down onto a hushed molten sea holding its breath. The beauty of life struck me a blow.

The old Jaguar sports car I was driving crunched to a stop on the gravel road. I watched as our father, the sun, flexed his lifeforce just for me, a pre-show of the day to come that he would share with us. Clouds queued up to glide and dream across an empty sky and play draughts with light upon the face of the sea far below. Your move, blue to black to purple.

I had been at an all-night three-day party. This is how it came to pass. In my little weekend business,

I got a call to move good furniture and pictures from a house in Dominick Street to a big estate in North County Dublin. The client, Mr Scott, was a well-known, rich, eccentric recluse. Dominick Street then was not grand but its Georgian houses once had been. It had once been des res. I knocked on the huge front door and stood back to look up at the gaunt, sombre facade with its high sightless windows. No man has ever built more gracious shelter than the early Dublin house.

Chains rattled. Heavy bolt slid back. Open. A big man, bald man, tall man, old striped pyjamas, frayed. Toast one hand, teacup the other, paper under the arm, bare feet, a beat of silence. Holding door with his foot. Balanced. This could go either way.

'Who are you?'

'Van boy,' I said. 'Across the street, around the world. Remember? My card!'

His hands were full. I hesitated. I put my card in the top pocket of his pyjamas. He burst out laughing, he roared laughing.

'Join me for breakfast, Van Boy. Nothing fancy, home-made bread from the Dainty bakery on the corner, courtesy of Mrs Shevlin, may the light of heaven shine on her. Marmalade with oranges kissed by the sun of Spain, rolled on the thighs of señoritas. Salted country butter from my little man in Mullingar, you can't beat the Mullingar heifer.'

We sat down.

'Tea? Milk? Sugar? May I call you Van Boy?'

I looked around. Soaring, perfect Georgian rooms. Peeling paint, furniture stacked, faded good Chinese wallpaper, high piles of books, mountains of newspapers, two motorbikes, engines, bits of engines, pictures along the floor, one huge Dutch seascape, a large pram full of files, its hood up. We sat in a nest carved out of the chaos on two deckchairs with an important early Irish table facing a south casement window.

The garden, a big wide Dublin garden. High old brick walls, the colour of young tobacco. A rude green sea of nettles down to a strong mews house, windows and doors gone or gaping. In the main door, a fat piebald pony with a newborn foal, her morning interrupted by me. She swished her tail and looked hard at me with eyes full of questions. I had no answers.

'The foal is Hi Ho after Tonto and Kemo Sabi, my heroes,' he said.

The sun had his hat on and came out to play around our feet.

'I have put your card up on my chimney piece, good start.'

A battered old silver teapot, proper china cup and saucer. He stirred his tea most carefully without touching the sides of his cup. It's hard to do, try it. He leaned into the silence and said quietly, 'Hitler had only one big ball.' More stirring.

He lay down his teaspoon with delicacy and precision. Soundless. I waited for more, there was no more. I stirred also quietly and also quietly said, 'Himmler had something similar but Goebbels had no balls at all.'

More silence. Had I passed a test of some kind?

'I hear you like good furniture?'

I was learning.

'I like your house more.'

'Clever dickie,' he said. 'I have dozens of them around the city. I too like furniture. I will keep you busy. The secret of keeping old houses is a sound roof. A gentleman must attend to his slates, his leadwork, his gutters. Look up, not down. Rain is the curse and blessing of the emerald isle.'

'But how do you heat them?' I said.

'Layers, darling, layers, as my mother said. Layers and movement and plenty of fibre.'

In my innocence I said, 'How can you have enough money to have dozens of houses?'

'A good question,' he said, 'making money and keeping money are two different skills. My ancestors before me were good at making money. I am good at keeping it. The trick is not to want more. Sufficient onto the day etc. Softly, softly catchee monkey. Speaking of money, how much are you charging me for this job today?'

'Eight pounds,' I said.

'It's not enough.'

He went to a big black handbag and took out a fistful of money and gave me twenty pounds.

'When you work out a price, double it. Charge more, work less. Some will pay. Select, say no, wait. Don't be afraid of being idle. That's when the money is made.'

A business course in one minute. He saw me looking at the handbag.

'My mother's. I have always run my business from it. I sleep with it under my pillow. The big pram holds my files and papers. The wheels, you see, handy, can be moved, no bother. Mrs Shevlin pushes the pram for me from house to house and carries my handbag. Instant office. Pity men can't push prams.'

'How many houses do you live in?' I said.

'Seven,' he said, 'I own thirty.'

'Why?' I said.

'I like the change of air,' he said, 'I go to West Cork for the summer.' There was no answer to that. I remained silent. As did he.

'You know my son, Baz, you have been to the ranch, our old home. He runs a commune there. His mother died, his granny left him a pot of money, he's gone native. Won't go to college, he is a hippy now. You know he's a mad bastard, weak in the head and strong in the trousers.'

'Different,' I said, fondling my twenty-pound note.

'Have you been to the parties?'

'Sort of,' I said.

'Sort of?' A small cloud hovered.

'I went for two days to a four-day party.'

'Where did you sleep?'

'In a pair of curtains, behind a sofa,' I said.

He groaned, 'My good curtains. What did you deliver to him in your van? What?'

'Early Japanese erotica,' I said.

'Dirty little brat,' he said. Baz was six foot three.

'Did you meet the girls from the local factory? How did you get on?'

'Like Quality Street, there are hard ones and soft ones,' I said.

Silence settled again. Time swayed. I may I have softened his cough.

'More tea, vicar?' he said. 'To business.'

He got up, took chalk from a drawer, wrote across three pieces of good furniture 'Loaner'. It's still on them to this day. The pieces I brought back had 'antichrist' sprayed across them. Again, still there to this day. Looks good, People ask.

I loaded up. He said, 'May I book you for next Saturday? Breakfast nine sharp. My little man may send eggs. Are you a boiled-egg man? I will ask the Dainty to make soda bread.'

'Yes please,' I said.

'Good man ... religious?'

'A daily communicant,' I said, 'I was an altar boy to a bishop.'

'Jesus saves,' he said.

Meanwhile, back at the ranch, a good small Palladian house settled nicely into its six hundred Irish acres, small river, a strong farm, as they say.

'Where will I put the furniture,' I said to Baz, who stood out in the yard wearing a long Moroccan shirt. Stoned, out of it.

'In the skip,' he said. 'Come and have a pale sherry.'

'Were you interrogated by the antichrist?'

'Client confidentiality etcetera, etcetera,' I said.

'Tied to a chair and battered? What did you tell him?'

'He knows everything. He's worried about you, Baz, you're not taking your medicine, drink, drugs.'

Baz said, 'Bugger that! Big party tonight, we have three kegs, get the Jag out and see what you can rustle up in young girls from the town.'

'What's the theme,' I said.

'Broken promises, that will sort the men out from the sheep.'

I saw a lamb sitting on my folded sleep curtains, taking a keen interest in all that was going on around him.

'Larry has not been well,' a pretty girl told me. 'I have been asked to mind him. I work here now.' Hello?

I got a small room in the servants' wing. The party was one of the greats. Mighty. A huge fire, huge crowd, at the bend in the river, by the millpond. Full trees burning, the night air sang of Moroccan woodbine, the babble of happy people, horses standing quietly at the edge of light, dogs and children ran wild. Farmers from miles around. Half the Bailey, West Brits by the yard, would-be rockstars, actors, barristers, Bengals, a good fiddle player, set dancing, swimming, local girls jiving to a boom box at a sub-party. Hurricane lamps hung in the trees, many candles, magic was in the air. The big house glowed at the top of the field.

I met Rosie. It was instant, rapturous. She took no guff, no prisoners. Rosie, Rosie, Rosie. Far into the night, I was drunk with twelve pints and shouting about inequality. She said, 'Shut up, you silly smoked- salmon socialist, and kiss me.'

I kissed her. She led me down to a soft bank on the dark side of the river. Careless whispers under a duffle coat. Soft lips. Gentle hands.

We retired to the servants' wing for three days and three nights. I left only to forage for food and drink. As my granny said, 'An empty sack won't stand.' Wise woman.

Baz was getting madder. He rode around the yard on a big grey horse with a gun and holster, with his shirt off. The noise of a nervous horse on the cobbles of a Georgian yard speaks of alarm and war. He took an axe to a door he thought was locked. Rosie went home to her mother, she told me I was wasting my life. She had a boy in the village, a qualified mechanic. 'He has prospects,' she told me.

Baz suffered from what he called 'the hiddens'. He could not tolerate people to look at him. When you spoke to him you had to look the other way. He looked back only through his fingers opened out across his eyes. He stayed in his room for days. He lived on pints, toasted sandwiches from the pub known as the Mutton

Dagger, whiskey and weed at night. He read poetry to girls and lambs.

Some days after the last big party me and some 'guests' still remained, sleeping in vans and tents. We were cooking rabbits we had shot and trout from the river over a big open fire on the terrace. We had bought two cases of cheap red wine. A girl ran screaming out of the woods.

'Baz, Baz, he's dead, he's dead.'

When I got to him, he was lying on his side in the water at the bank of the big mill pond. We pulled him out. He was not dead. We got him up to the big house on the bonnet of a Land Rover. They put him on oxygen in the ambulance, its flashing blue lights made the woods scary. He was gone for many months.

Mr Scott rang me and told me to clear everybody out and lock the place up, then to come and see him. Get the police, phone him and nobody else. I followed orders to the letter. We lit a big fire in the yard, burned all old tents, clothes, sleeping bags, two gipsy vans. Four vanloads of empty bottles to the dump. My sleeping curtains put back up. I heard the sound of a Hoover, hippies don't do Hoovers, I stopped it.

It took me and two labourers two weeks to clear the place. On the last day I stood in the yard and felt the shades of people who had lived here before us for hundreds of years. A time before factories, offices, shops, a time before going to work. A time when people lived off the land behind their walls. Many never left. I felt they had liked us being there.

As I was finally shutting the big gates at the entrance, a man passed leading a horse and cart of manure.

'I hear the big mad young fella went Bismarck. The land knows nothing, and cares less. There will always be manure,' he said looking at his load.

I drove the powerful convertible Jaguar hard on the winding back roads. Summer wind tore at my hair. A door in my life closed with those estate gates, I felt this was a new start, a new time, a new dawn. I was ready, I was strong, I was young. Waiting for the next door to open. It was my time. Life called to me, I would answer.

21
DODGE

Summertime. Quiet, warm, morning. Good-to-be-alive morning. Good-to-be-young morning. Frisky little breeze in from the sea, lazing in the sun outside the gang HQ, our much loved old Chevy. Idle chat, this and that, how's tricks, half listening. Watching a pilot launch butting hard down river against a chop. White water. A bone in the teeth, the old saying. A big blue funnel ship out of Baltimore, USA, hazy, low on the horizon, shimmering in the heat on the bay.

The yard deserted. All away, big job on. My father's car outside the office, funny that. Keys left in the ignition by the mechanic. Sat in, radio on, warm smell of good leather worked its old seductive magic. Soon the whole gang was in. Radio, cattle prices, the budget, distant wars. You need to keep informed.

Would it start, it did. It seemed natural that I should drive around in big, slow, walking-speed circles. No reason, but it was good. Tonto, the yard dog, sat in the middle, his disapproving look. I have noticed before that dog has good judgment. I should have listened to him. By the way, the real Tonto's horse was called Scout. Nobody knows that. Silver gets the limelight with that hi-ho thing.

A voice from the back. 'Let's go up to the shops, it's only at the top of the lane. We can buy custard creams for elevenses.'

Custard creams were the biscuit of choice for our gang. Made with milk, good for growing bones.

At the shops we met Skin's sister and her three pals. One a looker, but lippy. Her name was Tilly, like it, good start. It seem natural they would all pile into the back seat. It was compact, but the old Dodge was roomy. The squeeze was nice. Chatting, custard creams, romance in the air, where would you get it. As my uncle Ned says, 'Better than a kick up the arse with a snowy boot.'

Tilly said, 'Why don't we drive out to Dollymount beach for a paddle.' I told you she was lippy. What could go wrong, who would know, nip in, nip out, no bother.

I needed to see out the windscreen for the drive. Cushions and books from the boot lifted me up. I could see for miles in all directions.

We stopped at the chipper in Fairview. Nine singles, nine bottles of cider, Woodbines. More custard creams. Nudger sat beside me as I could not get the clutch all the way down. My beautiful assistant did a good job as I called the gear changes.

'I'm impressed,' said Tilly, 'Can I do the clutch on the way home?' Hello, lippy and pushy.

We kept the chips and cider till we got to the beach. The custard creams were hoovered.

'Hunger's mother,' Tilly said.

Along the coast road, nice and easy and slow. Radio on full, all the hits. Singalong from the girls, they knew all the words, how do girls do that? When a love song came on they all hugged and giggled.

We clattered across the old wooden bridge to the strand. I gunned the big V8 engine and raced full speed the whole length of the beach to the very end, the sea on three sides. I parked at the dunes, open doors, loud music, dancing. Then we sat around in a big circle, ate the chips, soggy with vinegar. I can taste them now.

The simple sun shone down on us that day. We knew this was our time, a time that would touch our hearts.

A paddle with Tilly in the quiet sea, soft sand between my toes. We held hands, then she kissed me. Oooh. I lost my socks, the tide had sneaked in, we were lucky to get out, water up to the doors.

Coming back up the beach I practised my sudden swerves, jamming on the brakes. Much screaming, girls liked being frightened, nearly turned over, they drowned out the radio. Seagulls, joggers, old people scattered. I drove one wheel into the sea, big spray, fantastic. Girls screaming off the screamometer. I think the boys were screaming too.

All quiet on the way home. Tilly again. 'We should finish this perfect day with an ice cream in the Broadway café.' Quick check, we had enough for four ices, so it would be multispoons and counting.

The king of the road, I turned into O'Connell Street, a guard in the middle of the road, arm up.

'Good afternoon,' he said 'And what is your name?'

'Cedric McGinty,' I said.

'Good man Cedric, you're a popular man, many friends, most of them in the back.'

'Yes, and no,' I said, 'We were at the Rosary and I'm giving these young ladies a lift home to their mothers.'

'You are a caring young man, Cedric, an example to us all. Can I see your licence?'

'It's at home being minded by my mother.'

'That's disappointing, Cedric, most disappointing. I was very much hoping you would have it.'

A bit of a wag, our guard.

'I suspect you are going to be with us for some time, Cedric, perhaps you should tell your young lady friends to go home to their mothers, they must be wondering where they are now that the Rosary is well over.'

All piled out of the car, Tilly squeezed my hand. 'Be brave for me,' she whispered. I could only hope she would not mention the bank heist we had discussed, should she be grilled by the police.

We were right outside the Savoy cinema, a long queue watched our unfolding drama with keen interest. A Doris Day picture, losers, a queue of losers. Doris Day, no way.

'Who owns the vehicle, Cedric?'

'My father,' I said and gave his name.

'I know him,' said the guard, 'A finer man never stood in a shoe, I'll give him a buzz to see can help with our inquries.'

He strolled over to the patrol car, the Doris Day'ers watched every move, this was better than the picture, that would not be difficult. He strolled back, a different kind of stroll now.

'Disappointed again, Cedric, disappointed again. Your father said his car was stolen by a common thief and we should apply the full rigour of the law. I'm going to arrest you both, now put your hands out for my handcuffs.'

We were cuffed, the queue goggled. I held my arms up to show my chains in the age-old gesture of defiance, a slave, his freedom taken. The Doris Day'ers gasped; they hoped the queue would not move now, there could be a shootout.

No shootout. We walked to the squad car. It's hard to walk in handcuffs, it's a balance thing.

Into the station, down to the cells. A small crowd of other 'clients'. All innocent men, all puzzled men.

'Why are we here?'

'I was in the house, I thought it was on fire, I was trying to help.'

'These pearls are a family heirloom, my sainted mother's.'

'He knifed himself to get me into trouble.'

The two guards called us into a bare room. One table, one bare bulb, no window, four chairs, one ashtray. Smell of damp, sweat, fear, vomit. A room for the fallen.

'Good man, Cedric, have you anything to say that I can put into my notebook?'

'I was in emotional turmoil, I was not responsible for my actions,' I said.

'Were you ever in emotional turmoil?' he said to the second guard.

'I was not,' said the second guard.

'Did you ever hear of another guard being in emotional turmoil?' he asked.

'I did not,' said the second guard.

'Do you know what emotional turmoil is?'

'I do not.'

Silence fell, notes taken, slow writing, scratching noise.

'What caused this emotional turmoil, Cedric?'

'My girlfriend, she told me she had fallen for another.'

'Ah yes,' he said, 'Young ladies can be fickle, Cedric, love can be elusive.'

I wanted to say he would make a good agony aunt. Or agony guard. Wisely, I did not.

'Broken hearts and stolen cars are strange bedfellows,' he said.

I remained silent. I knew from Perry Mason, anything I said would be taken down and used against me. Not a dickie, no fool me.

Here comes the night, coarse blanket, stinking pillow, an endless freezing night. Random shouts and screams. From the high window in my cell, I saw a weary old cardboard moon hanging on a string over a weary old Dublin.

Morning. A dirty grey dawn stained the walls of the cell. A ten-gallon drum of porridge slid across the floor. So old, so cold, so hard the big ladle stood up without touching the sides.

'Room service,' said a voice that banged on steel bars with a metal truncheon. Who knew policemen hand such an impish sense of humour.

Twenty persons shuffled out to the yard with high walls, the sweepings of a long cold night in the city when the drink wore off. No Doris Day here, oh no, they believe in the magic of the movies.

A stone-cold Georgian basement under the courts. Long stone steps up, we could hear the judge. His porridge too had been cold, by the sound of it. Not a happy camper.

Our names were bawled down the steps. We climbed up into the half-hearted light of a room built to give no cheer, no comfort, no hope.

My friend, the wag.

'I was attending to my duties, Your Honour, a large motor vehicle approached me, I formed a suspicion, which upon investigation proved to be correct. The vehicle had been purloined, the driver was underage, no tax, licence, insurance. The vehicle carried more than the permitted number of passengers, Your Honour, many more. There were young ladies present. Alcohol may have been imbibed. I deduced this by the lingering smell.' Perry Mason again.

The judge blew his nose loudly and looked into his hanky. The court waited in silence. He examined the contents carefully from different angles: clearly, they were not satisfactory.

'What's this about turmoil?' he barked.

'I was only messing, sir,' I said.

'I am not sir, I am Your Honour, we do not like messers here, do we sargeant?'

'No, Your Honour, we do not like messers here.'

The judge looked at me over his hanky.

'I read here, your lady friend left you for another, a wise young person, most wise. I think you are a gurrier, young man, setting out on a life of crime,' said the judge. 'Am I right?'

'Oh no, Your Honour, the scales have fallen from my eyes, I will knuckle down to my school work, no more romance for me.'

I had been given these words by a fellow 'client' in the cell.

'The car was your father's, I see, a most unfortunate man.' He has raised a gurrier, a messer and a thief: if you ever come before me again I will send you down, do you understand me?'

'Yes, Your Honour.'

'Probation Act, I see a woman weeping in the back of my court, your mother I suppose, go and beg her forgiveness, now get out of my sight. Next case.'

My mother and her sister bustled me out of the court, laughing and crying. Tears of joy.

'Go and stay in your auntie's tonight. Let things settle down at home.' They both hugged me together. I did as I was told; I was not looking forward to meeting Himself.

Two days later my father arrived. He took me by the shoulders. 'My beautiful son.' He crushed me in a bear hug so hard it hurt. 'My beautiful, beautiful son.' He held me with his hand behind my head.

'I told the rozzer to give you a fright, not to bring you to court.' He may have cried, I know I did.

He held me out again by the shoulders.

'You're a mad young fella, You're not a man yet, your brain is not switched on. I will sit by the watch fires in the night to see no harm befalls you as you grow, you are mine, my blood, my son. I am proud of you. Tell your mother I kicked you up and down the street.'

When he died, his world, his skills, his knowledge, his goodness was swept away by a world beyond his understanding. A world, more cruel, a world more selfish, a world not for the weak.

When I think of him, the strange and quirky comment of the wag policeman stands monument in the morning light.

'As fine a man as ever stood in a shoe.'

22
F L O

Hacking jacket, fitted waist, tweed, cavalry twill, brown brogues polished, always, always, a brightly coloured cravat. Thick strong black hair, glossy, combed back in the way of an officer of the British army. Meet Manfred Tussel. Vain. Tall, loud, clipped in that nearly rude way of his type. Felt he cut a dash, little did he know.

An antique dealer by trade, top end. Knew his stuff, born into it.

Some men go through life making things difficult with arrogance. Manfred was the commanding officer of that brigade. A charm bypass.

Like all bullies he sought out the weak, the timid. But the weak too can build their little barricades. Every day in every way they quietly, gently worked against him. He never knew and would never know, a little smile, a pat on the back, respect, would open that low gate in the wall and kindness would enter. It never did for him, he foolishly fought for every inch of the way.

He had one brilliant, original idea. Just one, but it worked. He ran his business from a lovely rambling honey-yellow Elizabethan manor house in the Cotswolds. It was surrounded by ancient tithe barns, yards, sheds. Here's the idea.

He opened only every second Saturday from ten till four. Not a minute more, set your watch. Open meant every room, every barn, every shed stuffed with good furniture, good pictures, all period, all 'right'. Chairs, tables, sofas, chests of drawers all piled high all for sale. Now. Right now.

Dealers, the public, all shouting, all drinking, all haggling buying and selling. Vans, trucks, loading, unloading. Wine, local ale, plates of food all day, no charge. The chair you are sitting on could be sold from under you. The picture you admired on the wall gone in one minute. People loved it, came from far and wide. It was famous.

Ladies formed indoor picnic circles sitting on the timber floors and sofas pulled together. All the gossip, dogs barking, yard full of trucks, vans, Ferraris, Bentleys, trailers. Some rode in on horseback from local farms. It was English, a triumph, a bash, a knees-up, a grand day out. Splendid fun, rock stars, celebrities, millionaires, all took their chances. It was rough but only pretend rough.

As the iron tongue of time told four all thrown out. An elaborate game, wheedling to stay.

'I just spent ten grand, you can't sling me out.'

'Watch me, bugger off.'

'Manfred, can I finish my bottle?'

'No, bring it home with you.'

They loved it, came back for more time and again, ten o'clock on the nail.

But as always in life, there was a better, sweeter, secret ticket. That low hidden door for the few. A VIP room inside a VIP room. A bigger laminate in the rock-and-roll trade, a nod, a wink, a chink in the curtain.

There was a discreet social cull. The favoured got a whispered invite to stay for a drink, 'supper' it was called. A word in the shell-like. The chosen few were complicit in this not-so-secret secret. Said their goodbyes, hung back. House yards, barn, sheds rapidly emptied. Then the few into the long kitchen, low ceiling, 500-year-old beams, priest-hole still in the floor. Long gleaming oak monastery table, many, many candles, full of wine. Big dishes of hot food. Full and plenty. Nothing fancy but that made it fancy.

Get your own, sit where you like, stand at the Aga, on the sofa. Back door open to the yard. Up close an old Land Rover, a shouting game of cards and spoof on the bonnet. Bottles of wine along the bumpers. Horses stood and watched. The rich at play, school chums, trustafarians.

'This '65 has potential.' A cheeky chappie punching above his weight. Whimsy meets pretension.

'I laid down fifty cases. I'll send one over to you for a slurp. My little man will be in France next week if you want more.'

'How's Maggie? More cheese? Did you buy that daub from Cravatman?' Our host's nickname for rich chums.

'Yes, flipped that offshore bond launch this morning, same day in and out, paid for pic and hols.'

'Did you?'

'Of course.'

Sometimes when we delivered, we stayed over to help on a busy day. We slept in a cottage on the farm. All day selling, helping ladies choose.

'You have to buy that little table, it's Irish, like me, and has good legs like me. Let me fill that up for you, Lady C.'

'Darling boy, you little rascal, kissy for mummy.'

'Mmmm.'

Guff, but good guff, our guff, we swam in it. They wanted more.

'You can do this,' he said to me. 'They like you, come and work for me full time, you're a natural. I'll double your money, house, car.'

'I have to look after my mother,' I lied.

He paid well, really well. We went home with bumper tips. We earned it, we were good, he knew, we knew.

His wife Florence or Flo. Funny, different as chalk and cheese. Knew the score, could play the game. These were her people; she too swam in it. She did a skit based on the old Andy Capp cartoon and his long-suffering wife, Flo. The old working-class drunk was always late home at closing time with a skinful, his collar sticking out. Flo opening the front door with a rolling pin, in her curlers and net.

'What sort of a time do you call this?'

I had to play the part of Andy with his white scarf and cap. Mumbled excuses. Bleary eyes.

'Wrong bus, leaves on the line, Bert's wife poorly.'

We had the cleaning ladies rolling around. But Andy and Flo always made up. She never hit him with her rolling pin. She loved him. Andy was effortlessly cool. The cleaners begged for more.

As soon as the gravel crunched under Manfred's Bentley, action stations, show over, boss back, rolling pin gone, curlers out, back to work. Flo did not do her rolling pin act for this Andy, only for us. There was no kiss and make up, not for him.

I gave up the van and got a proper job, did not see them for a couple of years.

Then this.

The Saturdays got bigger and busier. The drinking at the social cull supper went on all night. One night Andy and Flo had a blazing, drunken row. The house was full of guns of every type, shotguns, rifles, antique weapons, revolvers. A spectacular pair of Purdey duelling pistols, the finest made.

A drunk shouted.

'Settle it with a duel!' The table took up the chant.

'Duel, Duel, Duel!'

The fabled pair of pistols were taken down for all to see. A polished inlaid box with brass, dazzling scrollwork along the shining barrels, blued steel in the Damascus way. Tiny ivory ram rods, a golden powder horn, a row of shot. All made and fitted in shapes in green baize. A tiny, exquisite, perfect little world.

'Out to the yard, out to the yard, out to the yard.' The chant, forty people excited, banging on the table.

'This is how life at the top should be,' a man said. 'Twenty paces, Twenty paces Twenty paces.'

'Turn, turn, tun.' The crowd surged. The same man said. 'A night to remember.'

The pistols were held facing the sky, arms along the chest. Flo had had enough and dropped the gun, crying. Manfred smiled and as the winner held his gun out straight. It jumped in his hand. A shocking bang crashed around the ancient barns and the stones of the yard. A panicked murder of crows rose up in alarm, spreading fear and fright across the country. Flo fell, dead before she hit the ground. Straight to the heart.

The ancient powder in the muzzle had fired. Someone had put a shot in the barrel and left it.

Flo was carried in and laid on the big table. Dreadful silence. People slunk away. The yard pulsing with blue light from many police cars as Manfred was arrested. Dawn muscled in on the act.

He was charged with murder, convicted after a sensational trial and sentenced to twenty years in Wornwood Scrubs.

There the story ended, except it did not.

Three years later I got a call from dealers who worked with him. They needed a document signed; as I knew him best would I visit him in jail and get it done. I got a letter from the prison with a time and date. One man, no presents, twenty minutes, full search, no taping.

A big English prison would break a human heart and soul. The first thing you notice is no windows. Every brick every door is painted pea green. The pain of a fellow human creature held captive is beaten into every stone. Strangely, the guards are cheerful and kind.

'Manfred has been telling us all about you, he is looking forward to your visit. He is fond of you and sings your praises.'

'How is he?' I foolishly asked.

'Good as gold, good as gold. Doing an advanced carpentry course, a gifted pair of hands. He won't be short of a job when he leaves us. A lot of the lads will miss him. So caring, he gives classes in starting your own business. He was a successful man you know, a millionaire. He had a big house, servants, travelled the world.'

'Did he?' I said.

'I know it says "no presents" but I brought some chocolate and cigarettes. Would it be OK to give it to him?'

'No bother laddie, leave them with me I'll see he gets them. He gave up smoking, not much drink in here, going to become a minister. He has a lot of money you know, sold his big estate and business and wants to open a shelter for derelict men. He has formed a charity and given all his money away. Even our guvner calls down to see him. We are proud of him; he is loved in here and will be missed, especially by the weaker ones.'

I was shown into a long room divided down the middle with a metal screen and benches. Two other visitors, both women. Three men, prisoners, came into the room, baggy work jeans, fleece shirts between two guards, none of them my man. A small, stooped, grey old man walked over to me.

'Hello Cedric, good of you to come.' I was shocked to the core. This feeble person was the shell of the big strong man I knew. The big voice was now a whisper. He was smaller in every way, diminished, shrunk, dried out, a husk.

I could not speak, my voice failed me.

'I am sorry for what happened,' he said, 'I know she was your friend. I pray every day that I will die and be released from my shame, my pain.'

I spoke: 'I was asked to get you to sign this.'

My voice was weak and papery.

'They will make a lot of money from this, are you getting any of it?'

'No,' I said.

'Tell them I will only sign if you get a nice little house of your choice. Have you got a house, Cedric?'

'No,' I said.

'You are only the third person to visit me; looking at you I remember how much fun we had in Dublin and at my house, Flo begged me to give you a job. She was fond of you like a son. I have heard all about the Andy Capp running joke. I'm deeply sorry I missed that. I was a foolish, stupid man who did not know that nobody is impressed by what we take, only what we give of ourselves. Come back to me when you have a little house and I will sign.'

I got the house; a redbrick in a quiet Dublin street. It was a lucky house for me, he signed when I went back. On the morning of his release, he left the prison to thunderous applause in every cell, every block, every corridor. It went on and on as he walked across the front yard to the gate. The prison governor was there to shake his hand. An off-duty guard gave him a lift into town and left him at a small boarding house where a room was booked in his new name.

He did buy a large warehouse down by the river and left a fund to convert it into a shelter for those who had fallen through the net, the weak, the timid. It was to be called Florence House.

As soon as all was ready, he made his wish come through and departed this world by his own hand. An old man found dead in a narrow bed in a cheap boarding house. Move along, nothing to see here.

23
SWISS

I am Spartcus, I am Spartcus, I am Spartcus, bright-orange graffiti, aerosol-sprayed down each side of a forty-foot container. A bloodied sword the full length. The container sat in an abandoned building site, a burnt-out shell. Stripped of everything not nailed down. Steel fencing all around, heavily vandalized. More words sprayed, rude words, angry words, words of no mercy, words of no forgiveness.

Dumpers, bulldozers, diggers, burnt-out shells. Black hulks against a shy blushing evening summer sky. Dublin, inner city, early seventies. The past is another country. Welcome.

Inside the container four young men, early twenties. A full gym set up, cheap plastic tables and chairs. All four battle-hardened, tough, professional criminals. Hard as nails. Outside society, outside law, outside pity. To them life was a hunt, we were prey. Targets, sheep to be shorn, the enemy.

When they were working, no drink, no smoking, no women. Every man must run seven miles every second day, two-hour training in the gym, every day, no exceptions. No money to be spent except in Spain or Liverpool, their second homes.

Three-months break every year. Leave Ireland, stay low, stay separate, no contact, radio silence, rest, melt into landscape. Eat well. Make babies.

They were working on a plan to rob a shipment of 700 high-value trophy watches. They knew roughly when it was due. Inside information. A family man, caught in a filmed honey trap, a closet homosexual. Blackmail. Captured prey.

Plan called up two heavy motorbikes, already stolen, already stashed. Number plates, engine numbers switched. No trace. Handled only with gloves. Drop-off points scouted. High hedges, front gardens, safe houses. Stolen goods shipped out of Ireland in a load of hanging beef. Destination Amsterdam, biggest fence in Europe, codename in the trade 'good as gold'.

They did not do business in Ireland. Never carried, never touched stolen goods. Travelled only by ferry from Belfast. No ticket, no record. This is how the plan played out. No guns, never guns. Only because of much lower sentences if caught. They played the odds. The courts knew, they knew. A game.

At that time trucks leaving the port slowed down to let dock workers jump on for a lift uptown. A tap on the roof of the cab, slow down. Men jumped off along the way, shouted cheerio.

The goods had arrived, game on. The small unmarked van picking them up was clocked. Its roof was marked with a large chalk x while the driver was getting his dockets: 700 trophy watches in four unmarked carboard cartons.

Gangs of young boys swam in the Liffey on summer evenings. They were fearless. They jumped from the roofs of vans and cargo sheds into the deep water far below. It was dangerous, exciting, people gasped. Mothers who saw it hid their eyes and crossed themselves and hurried home to their children.

The boys that day were subcontractors. Brothers, friends, serving their apprenticeship, learning their trade.

A lookout in the cabin of a dockside nodding crane spotted the x-marked van from his perch high above the traffic. An old crane built by Stothert and Pitt, handmade, proper, old school. A thing of beauty.

He signalled ahead to the lifting bridge. A swarm of young boys climbed up onto the steelwork of the bridge and rained down pre-set milk bottles onto the road. All traffic stopped.

They took their togs off and hung out of the bars naked. A crowd gathered. Some laughed, some were shocked. The priest was called, they knew what to do with young boys.

Traffic backed up. People got out of their cars to watch the naked boys skylarking around the steel bridge. All eyes locked to the show.

Two heavy motorbikes cruised up either side of the line of traffic. Stopped at the car behind the van marked x. Got off bikes. One sprayed black paint across the windscreen, smashed the driver's window with a hammer. A hoarse whisper from a black helmet and mask. He held a hammer to his face.

'This will take two minutes, you will not be hurt if you sit quietly, got that?'

'Got that,' said the terrified driver. His wife started a scream, the helmet looked hard at her. She went silent.

The second biker had a heavy sledgehammer strapped across his back, warrior style. He swung high three savage blows and smashed the locks from the rear door of the van. Climbed in, took out four cartons, each biker put two in front of him on the petrol tank of the bike, roared away in opposite directions. The young boys vanished from the bridge, show over, send the priest home. Most people did not know anything had happened. The bikers threw the cartons over hedges into gardens of safe houses. Gone in an instant.

They rode to a lonely railway siding, cut the fuel lines to the engines, petrol gushed, set fire to bikes, helmets, leathers, gloves.

They strolled back to the river and stood in the crowd listening to the amused talk about the bold naked boys and the priest. Soon the road was swept clear, the traffic moved. Show over.

The police set up a roadblock and checked all vehicles passing. Optics.

Three of the men jumped onto a truck for a lift and passed the police in a crowd of men still laughing about the bold naked boys.

When the driver turned to the other side of the river, they were the last three men on the back of the truck. They leaned against the headboard with their backs to the cab and the wind.

The truck had a twelve-ton load of flour in gleaming white cotton sacks. They were stacked with a central walkway for unloading. The men were still on a high from the daring raid and did not notice the truck had turned into one of the roads with very low railway arches. The driver did not know they were still there. He drove on hard.

As they were shouting and laughing over the wind, they died instantly. They died laughing, died full of success, died full of youth. Looking forward to a long holiday in the sun. Making babies.

A spray of red splashed along the pure white sacks, three smashed and broken bodies fell into the narrow gap into the middle of the load. The truck driver headed for his yard to park up for the night, he and his mate arguing over the radio babble about Liverpool FC. Heard not a sound over the heavy diesel engine working under a twelve-ton load.

The driver parked up in the yard in a row of trucks, clocked out. Went home, another day.

During the night the watchman rang his boss to say the yard dogs were going crazy and waking the neighbours. On the third call, the boss got out of bed and came in. They turned on the yard floodlights and saw the blood on the tyres in the moonlight at three o'clock in the morning. The silvery light of the moon made blood black.

They called the police thinking it was a hit and run. Soon the yard was full of police cars, blue lights strobing across the trucks. The driver was taken out of bed and brought in by squad car.

He claimed he had hit nothing and finished his work in the normal way. He could not explain the pools of blood under his truck. Only after two hours, as dawn tiptoed across the old yard, a guard climbed onto the load and the truth was revealed. The guard vomited and was sent home in shock.

The fourth man did not get on the truck, the leader, the brains. When the story broke, he did not panic, did not run, stayed calm, stuck with the plan. Laid low. He went fishing for a few days on a quiet river in Wexford. When the media frenzy cooled, he had the goods collected and stored in Belfast.

They were shipped as arranged to the international fence in Amsterdam, to be sold across Europe. A man was sent to Berlin to close the deal and send the money home in a load of machinery.

It was divided up exactly as agreed, every penny correct to the families of all three men. All money from previous work was also divided. To each man his share. All proper, again old school. The container, all phones, all gear burned out. Scorched earth. Flame does not talk.

He went to Amsterdam for a year out. Learned German. Worked with the Dutch gang as senior planner. They considered him a genius at his work. A legend was born.

He never carried money, never owned a car, wore a cheap watch, his name in his world grew from that job and how he handled it. He was a local hero who lived in the shadows. He was nicknamed 'Swiss' from that day after the Swiss watch movement. Now he thought that was funny.

24

HA-HA

My docket said, Collect a fine George 1st, small breakfront bookcase. This is a rare and valuable piece. All glass is original, great care must be taken. The client can be difficult. Saturday 11 am. Address supplied. No helper needed. Client will help load.

'The client can be difficult' can cover a lot, but it did not cover this one.

I arrived on the day, on the hour. I drove past a lovely old ha-ha and parked in front of a strong eighteenth-century farmhouse in 'cared for' condition. A big prosperous farmyard graced with age and generations of work.

An Arab in full white flowing robe and gold head-band walked down the front steps and wished me good morning. He shook my hand. His was a hard-working hand with a tough muscled arm behind it. The Arab had an Irish country accent.

'Come and have tea and cake with me after your long drive,' he said.

We stepped into a low country kitchen, flagged floor, old range still lit, painted pine dresser full of good plateware. A proper big pine working table down the centre, sauce bottles lined up, brown and red. No guff, no dickying-up. You would like it.

A blackened kettle sang out from an old coal-fired Aga. The Arab took out a beautiful sponge cake on a glass cakestand and put it down on the table.

'It's for you,' he said. 'I bake once a week, cakes, bread, buns. I do enough for two deserted wives who live in the village. Sugar? You have broken the five-minute barrier, you did well.'

'Barrier?' I said.

'Yes, In not asking why am I wearing a full Arab robe in flowing white with a gold headband.'

'Now that you mention it,' I said.

'I am a cross-dressing homosexual man, no camping.'

'I see,' I said.

'Yes, I wear good ladies' clothes, but sometimes I go into character, which can last for weeks. Now I'm channelling Lawrence of Arabia. Strange, complex man, I think he was one of us.'

'Oh,' I said.

'I'm not a faggot. I am a good farmer, I run a tight ship here. I work hard and so do my men. I feed a lot of poor people in the village who depend on me.'

'I think you look terrific,' I said.

'Young man, I think we are going to be friends. Do you fish?'

'No.'

'Pity, I will teach you. My little river is tricky but can be learned. Our trout are the talk of the country. Let's get the work done first.'

He led the way to the front of the house, 'the good room', obviously not used. On one wall the little bookcase, the best of its kind.

'That's a good thing,' I said, 'it's a pity to sell it.'

'My family bought it new,' he said, 'I need the money, this farm does well, but I just paid off a big bank loan to cover death duties. I swore I would never go into debt again. The bank manager here is a vulgar oaf, I hated him and the hold he had over me. He waited for me to miss a payment. I need a new tractor, I need to work on the ha-ha and the yard. The old farm is part of my soul and every day I thank God I was born here. I spend all my money and love on it. I have a sailor suit; would you like to see it?'

'Yes please.'

His wardrobes (six) plus another room overflowed with expensive frocks, costumes, ladies' hats, many, many shoes. He took out the full-size sailor suit. It was based on the image of Edwardian boy kings with navy blazer, white trousers, double row of brass buttons, and medals across the chest. A round sailor's hat with a white top and long black silk ribbons flowing down the back. *Hero* in gold across the front, 'from the Players cigarette pack', he said. He took off the Arab headdress and put the sailor's hat on. He gazed at himself in the mirror.

'Divine,' he said.

'Divine,' I said.

'I know I'm no oil painting but still, we must work with what we have.'

'Do you like me?' he asked.

'Yes,' I said, 'you impress me.'

'I wish I had a beautiful son like you, but I never will. My fella is coming down at the weekend, I would love you to meet him.'

'Does he dress up too?'

'Oh yes. I have an Arab costume for him too. This Sunday we will go for a long rideout and have a pint in our favourite country pub, perhaps meet the hunt.'

'In the gear? I asked.

'Oh yes, I have lived here all my life. I am accepted, part of the furniture. They boast about me, they look out for me. 'Everything becomes normal with time,' he said, 'whatever normal is. I'm a local tourist attraction at this stage.'

'What does your boyfriend do for a living?'

'He's a plasterer.'

'Oh,' I said.

'I know what you are thinking,' he said, 'you are all in your little social boxes, not in our world. We have left all that far behind. We take each person for what he is and not for his social standing. I don't give a toss about that, if he is a good man, that's enough for me. Before we load up I want you to see me on my Arab steed.'

We went out to the stables. An old man led out a big gleaming black horse with alarm blazing in his eyes.

The old man then brought out a saddle and gear. The Arab was fearless around the horse and in total control. He crooked his leg and the old man gave him a lift onto the huge horse. Not a word passed.

He was a natural horseman, sat straight up and down. He spread the white robes out along the flanks of the horse and walked on. I caught my breath with the beauty of what I was seeing as they crossed the yard. He spoke low to the horse, which stood stock still, lifted one leg and curled it up in a pose, then the other one. All done slowly. A little show for an audience of one. I clapped.

'I would love a photo of this for my children,' I said, 'no one will believe me.'

'Better,' he said, 'bring them down with your wife for the weekend. I will teach her how to make the prefect sponge, every woman's dream.'

He got off the horse with grace and ease and stood beside me in the white robes. As he said, everything becomes normal.

'Let's get the bastard loaded,' he said.

The bookcase was carefully taken apart and each piece wrapped and tied into a double blanket.

For lunch we had his home-baked bread with a thick slice of cured bacon expertly cut from a full ham hanging from a beam in the ceiling. One of many.

'This butter has been made in the same way and by the same family for centuries on this farm.'

It was the best sandwich I ever had. A taste bomb!

'And to celebrate our new friendship, bubbles; one small glass. I don't usually drink during the week,' he said. 'I will send your wife a good cake, a loaf of my bread and a deep cut from this flitch of bacon. Tell her I'm looking forward to meeting her. Do you love her?'

'Yes,' I said.

'Lucky man. I will never know the love of a good woman. It is a loss and a sadness.'

When I finally drove away, I thought he would cry. I looked back to see a tall Arab in flowing white robes beside a shining black horse. He was waving. He stood in front of his ha-ha, with gently folded Irish fields and low blue mountains dreaming behind him. Lovely.

25

DUTCHY

Hard winter, black night, bitter cold, early start. Five in the morning. Up out of a warm bed, tiptoe out of a sleeping house. Put my work boots and heavy coat on outside door. Each house on the street holds its breath and keeps its secrets. Silent night air dazed with cold.

Two-day booking with a famous north-of-England antiques dealer for my van. A clearance sale of a big Georgian house one hundred miles west of Dublin.

Picked up my helper under Clerys clock. A silent young man who listened and learned. He had a dry sense of humour, missed nothing. He had the single most-prized asset, he was honest. He was as strong as a horse. In the yard one day he was on top of a ten-foot packing case, He stepped off and landed beside me as I passed, easy and natural. It would have killed most people.

We drove careful and slow between the hedges white with frost. The road ahead a lonely pale ribbon, our yellow lights a welcome relief. No traffic, we met only a police car. I waved, they did not. Hard men, watching too many gangster movies.

When we got to the estate, parked cars a mile back down the road on each side. Big turnout. People love to see inside these big houses as they die. Their power and mystery ebbing away. Crocodile tears. They had their hour in the sun. New kids on the block now. No airs and graces under an auction hammer.

We were waved through the gate as we had passes from the London auctioneers. Where a dealer's van was parked was important in the business of such a day. I bunged a fiver and got a good spot near the back door. Went to meet my man to get my instructions. I was to open bidding on cheaper lots to test the crowd. My customer, Shadwell and Sons Antiques, *If it's old it's ours*, would then take over. Mr Shadwell was old school. Six foot three inches, twenty-two stone, long red English face. The face that conquered an empire, and won the war. He wore a huge double-breasted suit, light gray with wide stripes. Size twelve, orange cattle-dealer boots, he had a good grip of the ground. He had what my father called a proper haircut, short back and sides. This meant cut tight to the top of his head, then a grey mop. Fashion was not his first interest.

He was called Flasher behind his back due to his party trick. He would hold open the huge double-breasted suit, wide on both sides, wide as barn doors. This revealed a series of pockets down each side. His proud boast was that he ran his entire business from the suit. Top three pockets (left) were banking with a different cheque book in each. Below that was correspondence, many letters held in the pocket with a row of bull clips. On the other side was accounts and below that, filing. All held in place with rubber bands and paper clips. Many biros. Many colours.

The last pocket was private and personal. As he was still seeking Mrs Right he told us this contained his love letters. Much sniggering. He was looking for a settled older woman, to date without success. As he drove a Rolls Royce and lived in a mansion, word in the trade was that he was picky. He told us he would only marry for love, but he remained interested in the ladies, many ladies. Especially the fuller figure. I was asked if I had any suitable aunties in need of a good husband.

The bank was the best part of the routine. At the back of his ample generous high trousers, held secure with braces (red), a deep pocket on either side with a secure zip. From these came a warm curved truck hubcap of money, large notes only. Dealing money, not for spending. The curve was snapped straight, a brick of notes folded sharp longways with the back of the first finger running down the inside spine, the notes cupped in the hand towards the wrist. Counting was done with two thumbs peeling off in a monkey (£500) per count. It was done at the speed of long practice in all weathers. He joked he could do it on a galloping horse in a gale. A handshake, money passed, deal done.

Inside empty trucks were used for reselling during big auctions.

I told my man that a German dealer had been pretending not to look at a good Irish lion-mask table I was loading. I was told to stand beside him at the bar. Sure enough, I was asked was the table 'right'. I said yes. I was asked was it for sale. I said yes. I had been told to ask a monkey profit; I told the German my boss would take a monkey plus two (£700) profit on the hammer drop. He said split, I said yes. I signed the German's card with our number and he paid me out on the spot. I went back to Mr Shadwell and told him I got the monkey plus one. I palmed him the money. He gave me a £20 tip and £10 for my beautiful assistant.

He said, 'Good lad, go back to clearing the rooms.'

Full room contents then were sold as one lot. I sold what we did not want to local trade. We kept nothing after the Regent. Bunce.

There was a chest of drawers in a back room I was not sure of. Rough as a bear's arse, a technical term. I turned it up to look at its bottom, something slid inside. I opened the drawer, a parcel made of old newspapers, the end of the first war. I poked a hole with my finger, little picture. I went back to Mr S, he said if I was not sure let it go, we had enough. I asked could I buy the little picture I had found for my wife.

He said, 'It's yours. You have worked hard for me today and made me money. You will get a big tip and as much work as you can handle. If you come and work for me, I will open a shop in Dublin.'

I said, 'It was only a weekend job.'

'Shame,' he said.

Break for lunch. Mayhem. Catering tent, 'Miriam's Fine Dining', formal, her doilies and settings soon trampled. Carefully arranged tables pulled together, many pints. Coarse laughing, shouted insults, old feuds, hand-slapping, dealing. Heaps of money. Argy-bargy.

'For the love of Christ, Mick, twelve pints.' Miriam gave up and sat down and had a drink with us. It went on all afternoon, dealers walking in and out of the sale with their drinks as lots called.

Mister Shadwell's size made a pint look dainty. When he got an audience, he downed the pint in one go, five seconds, his record. He bought a round for the whole tent, big applause. The auctioneer called for quiet three times over the speakers. He called in vain. The hammer rose and fell. No respect for history, no dignity now.

As I was driving, I only had five pints. We drove home with four rich dealers sound asleep in the back of the van wrapped in our furniture blankets. A year's wages for a day's work in their skyrockets.

I got home at 2 am so exhausted I could hardly climb the stairs. I took off my heavy boots and silently went into our moonlit bedroom. I slid into the scalding, delicious heat of a bed of a sleeping woman with two small children and a baby. The deep animal pleasure of just being alive with my little family all heaped together in our safe warm bed, a scene as old as mankind.

There is no more in life than I had that night. That wonderful night.

I woke with a Dinky car up my nose. I was part of a game of dare, a silent group of my children and their friends around the bed. So tired I could not move. My wife took the kids away and I slept again till noon.

I got up to a big breakfast, a pot of tea, papers bought, first day off in weeks, a day of rest. Fire lit in kitchen; I counted my blessings, lucky, lucky man.

'I bought you a present,' I said to the wife, 'it's in my work bag, open it. A mystery prize.'

She took it out wrapped in the old newspapers.

'Save those, I said, 'they are interesting to read.'

She opened it carefully and held the picture up to the light. My heart stopped.

It was a masterpiece, museum quality. Dutch still life from the golden age of the seventeenth century. A Dutchy in the trade. Curved peel spiralling from a lemon, a pewter plate, a pearl-handled knife, a broken piece of bread, a lit candle. No more. Perfect, exquisite. It radiated quiet beauty, importance, quality. It demanded respect. It held the innocence of all great art.

I carried it out in shock to look at it in the morning light. It was untouched with lovely dirt and grime from four hundred years in smoky rooms. It was signed, it was dated 1621. Its quality was miraculous. I spent the rest of the day just looking at it, children ran wild round me.

The oak panel it was painted on was cradled to stop it warping. It was dry as old bone. I put it high on a wall with orders that it was not to be touched, I went to work next morning, borrowed reference books on Dutch art so that I could tell the wife what her gift was. I read that only two Dutch conservators in the world should clean it, it would take months, cost thousands.

When I got home that evening my wife told me that her best friend Marian had been with her all afternoon. Marian had a sad life: she had married a violent man who beat her so badly he was jailed. When he got out, he abandoned her and her children and was never seen again. He sold everything they owned and left her penniless. My wife met her at the shops and paid for her groceries. I was not supposed to know. It was only a loan.

'Marian loved my little picture so much I gave it to her. We both cried with joy. She has so little and we have so much. I was so happy I could give my friend one good day in her life.' My wife said Marian was delighted and had 'gone home to clean it as a surprise for you'.

'You should not have done that.'

'Why?' she said.

'It's worth a fortune, the price of several houses. Big houses.'

'You should have told me, how would I know, you said it was just a little picture.'

'You have to get it back,' I said.

'I can't,' my wife said, 'her family have come round now and are helping her wash it. It was filthy.'

My heart froze.

I ran for the door and raced the car round to Marian's house. Her mother opened the door.

'You lovely man, what a kind thing to do, she's still crying, we gave it a good scrub, plenty of soap and water, it's sparkling now, not a spec of dirt. You'll be delighted. It's drying off now in front of the fire. It's been there for hours; it must be dry.'

I was too late. It was lying on a towel near the fire, the panel had already split. The intricate wood cradling applied to the back of the panel had sprung and come away. Flakes of paint stuck to the frame. It would soon fall apart. It was destroyed. A four-century time-capsule of beauty gone.

I had not the heart to tell them. I said I needed to take it into work for a while. I wrapped it in the towel and took it to the yard.

When I opened the towel all the paint came away and stuck to it. The bare panel had split open and the frame and cradling was a small heap of firewood. I closed it again. I could not bear to look at it or touch it.

I went into the garage where a brazier burned all day. I gently placed the frail broken wreckage on the flames. I held my hand in the smoke and begged forgiveness from a Dutchman's soul of four hundred years ago. A man who had given his life to the creation of quiet beauty. I whispered to him that all beauty is transient and all things must end. I hoped he heard me.

I cried. A mechanic put his arms around me and asked what was wrong.

'I was careless with a beautiful friend,' I said.

'Don't worry,' he said, 'there's plenty more where that came from.'

He was wrong.

As nobody has seen the picture, I never told a soul, it was a secret. Only one man knew: a Dutchman of four hundred years ago and the secret was safe with him.

I bought Marian another picture. 'Children playing on a beach.' It did not need cleaning. It's over her fireplace to this day. It brought her luck. She married a friend of mine who loved her. She was happy every day of her life from that day.

Every Christmas I get a card thanking me for the lovely picture. She whispered to my wife in secret that she liked it better than the first one but not to tell me.

26

TINKLE

Married, mortgaged, making money. Small children, semi-detached, semi-skilled, semi-settled. Still seeking those elusive stepping stones to life, that low door in the wall to the sunny uplands that lie just out of reach.

My weekly outing, The Bailey after work on Friday. Packed, pushy, perfect, young, old. No tourists then. A type, a tribe, each one knew the other, we just knew.

Met Julian in the crush at the bar. Heaving. Like many young men then, social barriers falling, background hazy. No visible means of support, man about town, tall, handsome, languid, a ladies' man. Glossy. Snappy dresser, a silk-scarf man.

'Bubbles, young lady?' his line.

'You missed it,' he said, 'a big Hollywood film, full crew, pie and pints during the week. Shooting in Ardmore and Wicklow, the director, stars, the lot.'

'I'm invited to a party tonight, bring a friend. Are you a friend? You can be my date.'

'Your beautiful assistant,' I said, 'I can't be home too late, told the wife I would do the shopping.'

'We movie people don't do shopping,' he said.

A quick pint, hit the road. His car, an elegant old drop-head Alvis, navy blue, gleaming. As always, carefully studied for social nuance.

'Mustn't try too hard, Prince Phillip drives one, Douglas Bader too.'

'Calls up Spitfires, England expects, a bit rattly, but solid. Old school. New cars can be a touch vulgar.'

A young fogey.

On the way he told me he had a date with the director's daughter, Suzie.

The film company had taken over a failed factory complex to the west of the city. Beside it, a sprawling farmhouse with extensions and sheds in the Irish way. The drive was full of trucks, generators, lighting rigs, limos, catering vans. The whole front of the house lit blinding white by movie lamps. A generator muttered and grumbled behind a hedge.

Front steps and hall, packed with people drinking. Movie people, pony-tail people. Expensive ski jackets, hats, tanned. Glamour.

In fact, there were two parties. The director had a loud twenty-strong VIP dinner party in the main sitting room. Location tables in a long row, all lights off, dazzling banks of candles, mountains of food, many, many bottles. Two tons of logs piled up on the floor. Blazing fire in an open hearth. Crew disco thumping in basement.

The director sat at the top shouting. The first time I saw fame and success draw into itself all light, all energy, all oxygen in the room.

My friend Julian air-kissed his date. Then, selfish, like all of his kind, went into the big room and left me standing. I'm alright Jack. I was embarrassed and turned away.

'Who are you?' asked an American lady.

'Sorry, came with my friend, now I'm going down to the crew disco in the basement.'

'Don't be silly,' she said, 'be my date. You can see my husband is surrounded by adoring fans.'

And he was.

'Do you think I'll be missed?'

She squeezed a chair into the packed table, slid half her dinner onto a side plate for me.

'The catering is too far away,' she said, 'fill up on bread and wine. Who are you?'

We touched glasses and talked for three hours. We talked of my hero James Joyce. I was telling her that he had only ever wanted to be a singer.

'He sang in an old hall near where I live, the Antient Smoking Rooms. He won a small prize. I stood on the stage where he stood and sang.'

A tone had changed in the room, a missed beat. I looked around; the director was listening to me, his audience left hanging. Flustered, I stopped.

'Keep going,' he said, 'I want to hear this.'

I went on.

'Nora Barnacle, the women he married, was a chambermaid in Finn's Hotel across Trinity College quad. She told him he was a better singer than writer. She never liked his writing. They walked to Sandymount beach, their place. Their shadows linger in every doorway in this city.'

'On my next day off will you show me these places?' he said.

'I will come too,' said the wife.

Then Julian pipes up.

'My friend sings a song that Joyce loved by Yeats. "The Sally Gardens".'

'Sing it,' said the director.

'Oh no, don't mind him, he's only pulling your leg. I'm a toothbrush singer. No.'

'Sing it,' the director said.

'Sing, sing, sing,' banged the drunken long table.

The candles guttered and shook.

I sang.

The director, unsteady, came round and hugged me.

'I will use that one day, see you at the smoking rooms.'

The dinner party was ebbing away. Julian said he would drive his date Suzie to her small local hotel. The party spilled out onto the wide, gracious, granite steps. We all stood in the sharp cold night air. A half moon below gentle clouds. The director, a big strong man, put his arm around Julian's shoulder and shook him as a manly goodbye. A strange, light pattering sound stopped all chatter.

Tinkling tableware, silver spoons, forks, knives, danced and sparkled a little fairy dance down the old steps in the moonlight. Tinkle, tinkle, tinkle. Little silver bells in the clear cold air. Tinkle, tinkle, a cascade of cutlery.

Think horror movie, freeze frame, lightning flashes, dagger held high to plunge down. A no-breathing, frozen silence. We could all now hear the innocent little fountain chuckling to its gold fish. An eternity passed. Julian took his coat off, shook it out. More silver bells down the steps. Tinkle, tinkle. He walked down among the falling silver spoons, got into the old Alvis, roof down, even in the cold. He drove to the bottom of the steps and looked up at me. I turned my back and walked into the hall. He drove away slowly carefully into the cold night, his red lights sharp in the dark.

A maid stooped to collect the fallen silver.

'Leave them, get rid of them in the morning. Never bring them into the house again. Get some cheap knives and forks in the town. I'm going to bed.'

A good small picture was also gone. William Sadler, a Royal Navy squadron at the Pigeon House when it was an English naval base in the eighteenth century. The gap on the wall had been covered with a family photo. It was found propped against the main gate.

Suzie said, 'Don't speak, not a word, dance, now.'

Down into the pounding music, pumping crowd, danced for hours, drank. Did the conga out into the garden and back again. Three times. A girl shouted, 'He sang a James Joyce song.' Fame at last.

Towards dawn Suzie's mother descended. Another problem. An Irish crew member had put LSD in the honey. Bad trip. Outside the house a mighty oak, three hundred years old, its branches pink as dawn tiptoed over the misty mountain tops. He had climbed the tree and lay still.

Showing off, I said, 'Leave it to me.'

I climbed up, it took an hour, we got him down. He was shivering. We put him under a blanket in front of the dying fire.

'I know where he lives,' I said, 'lend me a car, I will bring him home.'

The mother said, 'We won't forget this.'

The car was a little Mini-Moke, an open-top utility jeep built on a mini chassis. It had a green canvas roof.

Suzie and her mother came with me to help lift and hold the man. We drove into town on the empty dawn streets. Along the Liffey, the pitiless, blank Georgian windows of this city I love and fear.

Suddenly, he shouted and jumped out under the canvas he had opened without us knowing. He raced across the Ha'penny Bridge, gone. It crossed my mind to follow him as the Mini-Moke would easily fit. Thank Christ I did not.

I took them to an early pub on Capel Street. Foaming pints, seven in the morning, packed, singing. They could not believe it. They loved it. Brought the crew after the next night shoot. I left them there with two Dublin poets. Unpublished. Good luck with that.

At home I told my wife of my adventure with the movies. We were invited to meet the stars and bring the kids.

'But what will I wear?' she said.

'Don't worry, you will be the most beautiful woman there.'

'It could be a long night,' I told her, 'we movie people like to drink and sing in the early morning.'

27

QUEENIE

Invitation. Small, tasteful card. It said, The lady vice-captain elect at home for bubbles and dead things on toast. 6 pm.

Mrs O'Reilly, aka Queenie aka Mrs O, uncrowned queen of our street. Human dynamo, whirlwind, driven woman, natural-born mover and shaker, social alpinist.

A housewife married to an ordinary man. Today, with an education, she would be running a major corporation.

She lived opposite us. Our street the lower modest foothills of the social pecking order. Mrs O had given her life to change this natural order and drive us by force of her will into a world of sherry in the afternoon, bridge on Thursdays, good works for the poor; the needy, she called them. She loved a committee, she loved a meeting, she loved being in charge, she loved writing up her minutes. 'Stick to the agenda, darling.'

Her husband, Tony, the long-suffering, she called him. Had always played golf since a boy and supported

Liverpool United. He was an artisan member of his club, which meant an affordable fee.

Mrs O had started to play as a lady midweek member. Her latest social triumph won from years of four balls, frostbite golf, club outings, turkey tournaments, whist drives, bingo clubs, fundraisers, committees, tea and lady members' cakes.

Slowly, slowly, she rose in the ranks, fought in savage hand-to-hand combat, close quarters, in the trench warfare of lower-middle-class ladies. No mercy, no prisoners, winner takes all. I liked her. She was funny because she did not know she was funny, did not mean to be funny. She did not get her own joke.

Of course I went. She was modest, even humble in her hour of triumph. She said she needed to speak to one of my people re 'freshening up' the white lines of her reserved parking spot at the clubhouse. A nameplate perhaps, small, nothing. She said she would see me later in private. 'Details, pet.' There was no escape.

Tony was a commercial traveller, old school. He 'carried' a range of affordable (cheap) soft furnishings. Three-piece suites, loungers (a winner), knock-off Danish coffee tables, a range of 'paintings' depicting the changing seasons, limited edition. Sometimes seaviews signed by the 'artist'. Fitted carpets, 'wool with a nylon mix, fully tufted, long-life luxury', his opening line to housewives when he called to measure. 'Would you like your underlay felt?' Ikea before it was invented.

He worked long hard hours. Monday morning, before the streets were aired, he said, on the road to his patch, all along the west coast of Ireland from Cork to Donegal. Six calls a day everyday, never give up.

Came home late Thursday. Friday rest. Saturday his day. Golf club all day, played a game, boozy lunch, poker, pints, pals, old cronies. Match of the day, thick as thieves. More pints, tales out of school. Shtumm.

His trademark his blazers. Double-breasted, four gold buttons in a square, anchors, coiled-rope surround. Range of shades, burgundy, pastels, beige, purple, tan, green, light and dark. Pride of place, club outings only, his best navy blue with club crest, his heraldic device, he called it. Latin motto *Nil desperandum carborundum*. Don't let the bastards grind you down.

With these he wore cream or white trousers, turn-ups, sharp crease, striped shirt, club tie of course. Selection of gold tiepins, a favourite, riding crop, curved and coiled.

Buffed brown slip-ons, American brogues, he call-ed them. A small chain across the foot. Natty, nifty, neat. Not a man you would miss in a county town in February.

Frank Sinatra, his idol, his party piece 'I did it my way'. When he sang this he got his audience to stand and belt out the last line, 'I did it my way.' Leave them smiling, a crowd-pleaser.

He was heckled, get off the stage, he gave it back, Teflon. Even his friends said he had a neck like Lester Pigott's mickey.

He spoke of empty winter country-town hotels. Only guests commercial travellers. His road friends, he called them. Special rates, the full Irish, pints with the lads, grim TV lounges up and down the west coast. Hall lights on timers. Sometimes, a sly bonus, a packed lunch to a favoured guest. I asked him once what was in a packed lunch. 'All your heart could desire,' he said.

I asked him was there ever any female company in the long lonely nights away from home. He leaned in, looked over his shoulder, put his finger along his nose. 'What goes on the road, stays on the road.' We both knew he would never look at another.

Mrs O's fevered military planning for her inauguration was thrown to the wind when the scarcely believable news broke: the lady captain had stepped down due to a sudden serious health scare. We were now talking lady captain and not vice lady captain elect.

A new ball game, a different league, playing with the big dogs. Now talking a marquee (300-seater), full band, Rory Rogers and his Ramblers, a tight, classy combo. Dress codes, order of speeches, seating plan, table placements, flower displays, menus, inviting other lady captains, parking protocols. On and on and on. Heaven, heaven, pure pure heaven.

My to-do list included my car I had bought when I made some money, a five-year-old Mercedes, light blue, top of the range, a looker, all extras, leather of course. Maybe old but good. She said it lifted the tone of the whole street.

My job, drive her and two 'assistants' to the event. I put my foot down over wearing a peaked cap.

The street, a disturbed beehive of garden-railing meetings. Women in groups, forming and reforming. This was big big big. The green eye was present.

Tony and me went for a quiet pint in a rundown, empty, dusty pub at the end of a sleepy Georgian street. Full of shadows, full of shades, wise old barman, doing the pools, seen it all, give me a break on his face. A shaft of sunlight peeped in the door. No tellies here, no anything, just drink. They tried nuts once, the whole box stolen, never again, stick to your knitting.

Waiting for two creamy pints to settle, this from Tony. 'When we are alone, I'm the boss, she likes that, wants it, she does what I tell her, she's meek. She asks my advice, she packs my case for the road, little notes in my pockets, sales tips, keep it up. She polishes my shoes, fills my flask, presses my blazers, shirts folded as new, one a day. I know you laugh at my blazers but we are a good couple. We are happy. We could live on the smell of an oily rag and did for years. We wish each other well. We are a generation that does not say *I love you* at the drop of a hat, but we do. She is my whole life and I am hers. We would be lost without each other. There would be no point in living without her. She holds my hand in bed till I fall asleep.'

'Lucky, lucky man,' I said.

'Don't ever let her down, she would die for you. She wants to impress you, be careful with her, she is not as tough as you think.'

'I know that,' I said.

The barman said, 'Do you want to listen to the match on the radio?'

'No,' we said together and drank our pints in the ticking-clock silence. A little outing long remembered.

The big day. Merc, waxed, a gleamer, hoovered spotless. Tyres to black. On the hour the golf bride emerged to a blustery day. Neighbours stood in their gardens, took snaps when snaps were snaps.

She was magnificent, epic, glorious to behold, radiant. Her hair spun to a bronzed highlighted bouffant. Her lips a racy-red sports car. Her eyes shadowed and blued to Cleopatra and her Nile. The frock a shimmer of blue ice. Made by many local hands, many fittings, many group consultations. A wasp waist, she had not touched food for weeks.

Club house first, drinks, little red umbrellas. Then the marquee, some milling around. The Ramblers noodling light, audible wallpaper, their power caged for later. They were a seated band, when did that change? Discreet pints under each chair, a round tray of drinks when needed from old fans.

The horn section, one man. Sax, clarinet, occasional trumpet, an all-rounder. Drummer, a famous comb-over, 'work with what you have'. Slap double bass, old and tired. Keyboards, Ozzie and his big organ, band joke. Young guitar player, throwing shapes, bit of a show-off, perhaps not a keeper. Anto, the leader, cool as cool at the mic, finger-clicking time, scoping the audience. He could wear a suit.

Seating began, follow the plan. Cascading importance down from the star. Then the first surprise, Anto into mic, 'Mrs O will now lead the floor.' Gentle applause. My cue, my secret, long planned. I stood up and led her out into a gentle waltz. Ooohs and aaahs, murmurs from mothers. New suit, electric blue. Mohair. Sharp.

We glided to the music. I felt something break under my hand. I watched in silence as her dress slowly slithered to the floor. It picked up speed as it settled as a ragged blue circle around her kitten heels. I looked into two large breasts, then looked down. Horror heaped on horror, I saw only tiny tiny pink knickers. Pink tiny little bows.

To their eternal credit the Ramblers played on, the tempo faltered but they goggled and played. In shock, I could hear my heartbeat and the blood running in my ears. I put my arms around her to protect her, she bent down, both knees together out to one side in one gracious and decorous movement, gathered up the frock and held it to her body. She said calmly, 'Take your jacket off and put it on my shoulders, no sudden moves.' I did as I was told. She said, 'Put your arm around me and walk me to the ladies.' Again I did as I was told.

The band played on. I went and sat down in silence, people looked down into their drinks, not yet ready to talk.

Tony rose up. Cometh the hour, cometh the man. He strode across the echoing dance floor to the ladies, three hundred pairs of eyes on stalks, pin drop, band finally faltered and fell silent.

'Send her out,' he said. Time passed, she came out, head low. A scarf held with a Celtic cross. He took her by the hand and together they walked across the dance floor. You could hear shoes squeaking. Into the mic, this. 'Good evening, you do us a great honour to be here, my wife, the lady captain would like to say a few words.' Thunderous applause, he handed her the mic. She spoke. All fancy notes gone, it did not matter what she said, they loved her.

Tony, a newborn star, a hero. John Wayne could not of done better. He was legend for that day's work. I got the nod to bring her home. Slipped away.

In her empty house she said, 'You must be starved, Billy no dinner.'

'I'd eat a nun's arse through a chair.'

She made egg on toast and a big pot of tea for the two of us. We wolfed it down surrounded by flowers from fellow lady captains. 'You were great,' I said. She took my hand and cried her heart out. I held her in my arms until she stopped. She sobbed. 'I let Tony down, I let Tony down.'

'Tony was proud of you, what a great man you have there.'

Years past, many years. We moved away, we kept in touch. Lives slipped away as lives do. Forty years later, one of her tasteful notes. 'I am dying, I want to say goodbye to you.' Still the same house, the same big extension she was so proud of. She had whipped those builders into shape, the architect too.

Tony long dead. The meeting carefully staged, the lounge (front-room) curtains drawn, lights low, nice small fire. I was shown in, left alone with her. She sat straight up, pert. Black dress, silver brooch, pearls, hair channelling the Queen. Feet together neat, prim, ladylike, demure, her hands loosely together in her lap, but out to one side. As always, planned. No guff, straight in. 'I always wanted to impress you, because you impress me.'

'Tony told me that long ago,' I said.

'I am looking forward to dying, I will meet my Tony again. I want you to give me a small kiss on the cheek, walk out that door, don't look back, I want to cry alone, I will miss you.'

I did as I was told as usual.

I did not go to the funeral a week later. Huge crowds filled the streets around the church. She had touched many lives, many hearts. I knew that when the priest went into the sing-song about eternal peace, I would think only of tiny tiny pink knickers with bows and laugh out loud. Not good for a lady captain and not good for one of the greatest people in my life. Respect.

28
ARCHIE

Small people seek each other out and pair off in marriage. It was always this way. Natural.

Standing outside an old shop in the Liberties, a little elderly couple shuffled slowly down the lane towards me. The lady was pushing a pram, a good pram, good make, Silver Cross. Chrome springs, cream tyres, navy blue canvas hood up. Smart. Classy.

They stopped to look in the window of the shop.

'Turned out nice,' he said.

'Oh yes, the sun on your face is a blessing,' I said.

'A treasure,' he said, 'we should never be off our knees.'

We three and the pram stood in the kindly sun and treasured for that little moment the gift of light, the gift of life. We were content. In that strange human way, we three knew that we would like each other, and we did.

'I often see you round here,' he said. 'You're from that rock-and-roll place, you must be up all night, I hear you're a bit mad.'

'Don't believe all you hear,' I said. 'Not a bother on me, easy and slow, that's me, easy and slow. That's how I kept my looks.' The little woman laughed.

'Go on you,' she said.

'Go in and get the rashers,' he said to the wife. 'Streaky, tell the man we knew his mother, a lovely woman.'

'Tell him to give you student discount,' I said.

I turned to him.

'Streaky, why streaky?'

'Value,' he said. 'The pension does not go far. I can't work anymore, my fingers are sore with arthritis.'

'What do you do?'

'I was a signwriter, I did a lot of the shops around here before the plastic. They used to call me Shademan, I could make my letters float off the fascia board. In the fifties we often used gold leaf. Pure gold in thin sheets. It came in little books, like a prayer book. It rattled when it was moved, like a bad chest, lasted for hundreds of years, did you know that?'

"I did not,' I said, 'before the plastic?'

'Now you type in words and a computer spits out your sign in two minutes, but it's dead, it doesn't float, each one identical, flat, plastic. My trade is gone, my world is gone, soon I'll be gone.'

'The baby is very quiet, is he asleep?' I said.

A silence, a pause, a beat of time. I waited, then this.

'There is no baby,' he said. 'He died years ago; he was two years old. Archie was his name.'

'We come from round here, just over there. Got one of the first Corpo social houses, out in the country then, bathroom, garden, grand, but we never settled. The wife said the country air was bad, different, that's what killed our baby, the bad air.

'We come back every Saturday to see our old neighbours. We bring the pram, she likes to think Archie is asleep in it. It makes her happy, makes her feel like a mother. That little blanket is changed every week, that's his rattle, his picture is under the pillow.'

Silence. We both stood and looked in the shop window. The pork butcher in his white coat, the little woman, other customers, butcher wagging a string of sausages, laughing. Us outside, no sound, a silent movie playing. Sadness stayed outside the window on its silver springs, hood up.

'You are breaking my heart today,' I said. But I had an idea.

'A famous painter comes to my place with the rock stars, he is a gifted man, a good man. Bring me the prayer-book of gold and a photo and I will get him to make an image of Archie in the gold in the style of the German artist Klimt. We could put it in a small glass case on our wall beside where you came from down the lane.'

'No wonder they think you're mad,' he said. The wife came out of the shop, excited, 'I got a student discount because of you, he sent you out a pound of best sausages.'

He did not mention what I had said to the wife. We parted and agreed next time they would come to a rock show if it was not too loud.

Some weeks later, I got a letter, beautifully written in a copperplate hand on fine white paper. It said the wife would prefer to remember Archie with his pram and blanket. Enclosed was a square of gold leaf. It rattled like the bright shiny paper from a sweet when you smooth it with your nail.